Arrows & Angels

Enlighten Series Novella

Kristin D. Van Risseghem

Kasian Publishing LLC
P.O. Box 211205
Eagan, MN 55121
www.KristinVanRisseghem.com

Cover design by Angela Fristoe, Covered Creatively
www.CoveredCreatively.com

Author photograph by Jessica Krueger Photography,
www.JessicaKruegerPhotograhy.com

Formatting by Jaye Cox
Formatting the Affordable Way

Other works by

Kristin D. Van Risseghem

Enlighten Series:
Swords & Stilettos (Book One)
Daggers & Dresses (Book Two)
War & Wings (Book Three)

Novellas:
Fires & Fairies
Arrows & Angels

Short Story:
Poisons & Princes

This book is dedicated to the ones who are no longer with
me, wherever you are.

May you always be watching over me. You are in the best
place now; in God's loving arms.
As you wait for me to be with you again,
know that you are in my thoughts.

May the angels stand by your side
as you become my guardian angel.

I will remember the great times spent together,
the smiles we've shared, and the funny stories told. The
sound of your laughter rings in my heart.

Know that I miss you, but I will endure.

I will survive.

And until we see each other again,

Life is Good.

Part 1

One

The Archangel Michael appeared, regal as always, on the top step of the palace balcony overlooking Heaven's meeting square. He paused, his eyes roaming over the crowd. Dressed in a deep blue, gauzy robe, his feet strapped in golden sandals, he descended the white marble stairs with his magnificent gray wings extended. His hand glided down the solid gold banister, a faint smile on his face.

"I seek volunteers. The human species and not the dinosaurs will soon rule the Earth. The humans, or Ordinaries as we refer to them need our help." His smooth voice projected over the assembled guardian angels. "The Council of Angels has requested we disperse to the Earth realm and watch for the birth of an Ordinary child. The fairies have proclaimed that an Ordinary girl will unite us and stop Armageddon. I met with King Oberon of the Summer Fairies' court to glean any additional information. All he shared was that this human girl will be special. People will flock to her. She will be one with all Enlightens. Her task will be to get them to join her and stop the first fallen angel's escape from his current prison and bringing Armageddon."

I looked around Heaven at those attending the meeting. Most of the Guardian angels had answered Michael's call. The variation of wing colors took my breath away. Like a snowflake, no two wing shades were the same. The vibrant hues stood out even more against the whiteness surrounding us.

A calm serenity washed over me as I listened to Michael's voice. There was a pleading in his tone. Something I never heard before. The moment he said the word "fairy," a vibration floated across my golden wings.

"No one?" Michael asked. "It is your duty to watch over and protect the humans. It is what you were created for." He scanned the crowd. "You're going to deny your responsibility? I understand your hesitance to volunteer to travel to the Earth realm, when many of you have always guarded humanity from the safety of Heaven, but this is critical to both our and the human's existence. I ask that you travel to the Earth's realm and monitor your assigned child so we can avert Armageddon. If nothing arises by the time she turns eighteen, you'll then be tasked with another. Until such time as *she* is found."

I frowned. The tranquility I felt, and the constant hum from the choir of angels, pushed at me. I couldn't fathom ever leaving here—or Him—and felt sure the others shared my opinion as no one offered to go. Some of the angels in the crowd bowed their heads, dodging Michael's probing eyes, while others wrapped their wings around themselves, shielding their bodies from his deep stare. Being an Archangel, he could see through their tactics.

The vibration I felt in my wings moved into my body. A spark flared in my soul.

Then, my arm rose. "I'll go as He wishes."

"Thank you, Kieran." Michael nodded. "Since you're the first to volunteer, you will be the lead angel and report directly to me." More hands slowly ascended, until a couple of dozen were held high in the air. "Carver, Trinity, Harper, and Nishan, as area lieutenants, you will convey all information to Kieran. The others, please sort yourselves into four groups for your assignments. Should you find any indication a girl has been born who may be who we're looking for, let your area lieutenant know. The rest of you are dismissed, for now."

Some angels walked from the square, while others simply disappeared. They didn't want to feel Michael's disappointment any longer.

"Each of the two groups will take an area of Earth." Michael waved the leaders closer to him as he opened his palm. A sphere appeared. "Carver and Trinity, you are assigned to the western region. Harper and Nishan, the east." He pointed to the land masses. "We don't have much to go on and I don't know what century she will be born in. But upon her birth, the gates of Hell will open and unleash masses of demons who will pave the way for Sammael's escape the day the girl turns eighteen."

Michael drew in a breath, even though angels didn't need to breathe. "He will bring Armageddon. So watch and learn as much as you can. If you prefer to remain unseen while you keep watch of your area, you may. Confirm the baby's details with your lieutenant immediately, if a potential candidate is found by your angel group."

My arm rose again.

"How, you wonder?" Michael continued without taking my question. "You'll know. Believe me. You are Guardians and He has created you to protect against evil. As such, when someone is destined to do extraordinary things, you'll instinctively be compelled to do everything in your power to protect them."

When he didn't elaborate further, I along with the other lieutenants took it as a cue to leave.

"Kieran, please hold. I want you to go where you think you are needed the most. There's is nothing else I can share with you to assist with the preparation for this task. But know that I'll always be here for your questions. The Council has requested I mentor you. They see great talent in you." He placed his hand on my bicep. His touch soothing at first, then my skin under his palm warmed. When he removed his hand two silver iridescent wings with a golden triangle in the center had appeared on my bicep.

I ran my fingers along the edge of the Triquetra symbol and it disappeared.

I nodded to Michael and took one last look at my home, searing into my mind the massive building with towering white pillars, floating pathways made of stone and surrounded by a thin layer of soft white light. That was how Heaven looked to me. I didn't know what picture others had created in their minds. It had never occurred to me to ask anyone before, and now it was too late. I'd be gone for at least eighteen years. Possibly longer as I moved from one potential girl to the next.

I wondered how He would let us know if the girl was the one foretold. He could have the earth tell us. We could be drawn to her. I guess it really didn't matter how he let us know in the end.

"And Kieran?" Michael asked, breaking into my thoughts.

"Yes?" I held my breath.

"Demons will be hunting for her, too. Those who want

to create chaos and death will work with them. Their numbers are currently low, but I fear as the time progresses and the Ordinaries population grows, so too will their numbers. As long as the demons know this girl exists, evil will attempt to destroy her and stop the prophecy. I don't know what forms the evil will take, so be diligent and stay safe. Sammael is clever. Even caged, he still wields enormous power. Do not underestimate him."

"I won't." I drew my wings around me. "How will we know our assigned child?"

"Their soul will call to you. You'll have an inner pull that will lead you to them. This is your first time on Earth, yes?"

I nodded.

"You'll need to acclimate to the surroundings before you are assigned a child. So for the first few rotations, you will only observe. When you believe you are ready, return to me. We will discuss what you've seen. You will have to learn much, as your time there may be extensive. I didn't want to discourage the others from the mission, but I feel the girl we seek will not be born for a long time. Centuries even. But I could be wrong." He placed his arm over my shoulder. "You will not be tasked with a child every cycle. My inner self tells me there is something special about you, Kieran. I believe you will be a great Guardian angel."

I drew a deep breath and nodded, absorbing Michael's soothing aura.

"I'm glad you volunteered, Kieran. I have made the correct choice in making you the leader. Something tells me you are destined to be the angel to find her. I cannot see your exact future, but I can see things that may impact your future." He scanned my body. "Your appearance will do you well. I think the humans will find you pleasing to their eyes."

Time in Heaven was not measured, as angels had eternal life. Many were still as youthful as they had been since the beginning of creation. Some angels considered me young since my face was like an older teenager, if you counted the ages of humans. While some angels changed their appearance as often as the sun rose, I kept my blond hair and blue eyes. I thought those colors went well with my fair skin and golden wings.

"Your lieutenants will be able to hear you, and vice versa no matter where you are on Earth," Michael said. "So if problems arise, you'll know about it, and then so will I. I'll help you as much as I can. This task may be lonely at times, but remember He is always with you." He embraced me, looked me in the eyes, and nodded. "You'll figure it out."

And then, I was dismissed.

What had I gotten myself into? I'd never left the safety of Heaven. I'd never been away from Him. I've never even had the inkling of a need to be anywhere but here. And now I'd be gone for who knows how long.

I wasn't sure what had made me raise my hand to volunteer, but something had. Maybe He made me do it, and I was here for a greater purpose. Who was I, a lowly servant, to question Him?

Two

Fifteen hundred and eighteen

I knew nothing of Earth or its occupants. Other Guardian angels observed the new species of *Homo sapiens* when they first walked the Earth, but I had no interest in them. My lieutenants told me stories of cave dwellers, fire and breathtaking landscapes. And that's what drew my attention. Nature.

This task had me doing many new things. I still didn't understand why I had raised my hand. As I floated down from the skies, massive animals and very few humans roamed the lands. Those who did, lived in packs.

Floating from place to place, figuring out what plants,

trees, and lakes were made of helped pass the days. While I had no charge to watch over—there was much to learn—I gained knowledge of time, the changing of seasons, and the concept of night and day. As time passed, the large creatures no longer inhabited the lands, making way for more and more Ordinaries.

I had taken to heart Michael's advice. In time, I loved the views: cascading mountains, dry deserts, and vast oceans. It was seeing these different landscapes that drove me to explore the Earth and exactly who and what inhabited it, even though none of the humans saw me. I felt no urge to meander physically on the land. I preferred to remain invisible and float on the breeze. Each of my lieutenants oversaw their areas with little complaint. They checked in and informed me that none of their charges were the one whom we searched for. Girls were born and died, many before the age of eighteen.

Eventually, I wanted to experience grass under my feet, the sun on my skin, and the wind in my hair, as the Human's did. When I finally materialized so the humans could see me, the Earth was too loud for my ears. I cringed. Beasts tore each other apart for food. The humans gathered what they needed to survive, traveled the land in search of their next meal, and slept when they could. Their lives never deviated. It was mundane, actually.

My travels between the extreme hot and cold

temperatures didn't bother me, since I felt neither but I could if I wanted to. What I did enjoy was the wind that would sweep across my face and feathers. It gave me the desire to fly, to feel the jet streams under my wings. And then I heard a voice.

"Kieran, go to Egypt. You will know of the girl when you near Nile Delta." Michael's strong voice sounded in my mind.

As Michael directed, I floated toward the city. Something pulled at me. Small dots littered the landscape as I approached. They were huts on the sand with dark-skinned people milling about. A mighty river ran across the countryside near the city. It provided the humans with nourishment, food, and other necessities. I needed to understand these new surroundings and learn the ways of this vastly different culture to that of the people I watched who lived in the caves. The language and actions of these humans baffled me. I'd have to study the words they spoke and the symbols they made on walls.

But there was an evil here, someplace. I could feel it deep in my wings.

Remaining invisible I landed next to a small child who ran around the banks, near her mother, who was washing rags in the river. The woman scrubbed and then laid the material on a rock to dry in the sun's heat. Sweet giggles filled the air. The little girl's smile was infectious and other children flocked to her.

She was somehow special.

Days passed and the humans did the same thing every day. The men would go to work on the triangle building. Large boulders would be cut, polished and then hauled into place. It took all the men to move one square-shaped rock. They labored from sun up to sun down.

The women cooked, cleaned, and did the washing. The children helped their mothers. They sometimes had time to play after helping the women who tended the fields and grew food.

Once a week, a delivery cart would be pushed down the hill from the temple and distribute one loaf of bread to each family. They lived in harsh conditions, with scorching temperatures during the day, huts that didn't provide much shelter in the extreme cold night, and ate very little of substance.

I watched as the self-proclaimed leader of the land lived in a solid stone building, which was much cleaner and grander than his subjects. He called himself a Pharaoh. He had fine clothes, more food, and didn't work. It was he who ordered a temple to be built and declared himself a god.

But I knew better. He was no god. My God wouldn't let his children suffer in a way that broke my heart seeing them in bare living conditions.

As months passed, the girl grew older. At twelve she was more well-spoken than those many years her senior.

Young and old humans called her charismatic and many stopped to hear her speak. Late night meetings began to take place with her taking the spotlight. Hushed whispers echoed throughout the growing community.

The people's poor living environment worsened, but that didn't break their spirit. A man spoke out against the pharaoh. He refused to worship him as a god and encouraged others to follow his lead and worship a different, more merciful god. The girl listened to the preacher and rallied the t families who were hesitant to join the rebellion.

To quash the uprising, the pharaoh dictated longer labor hours for the men. He disbanded all gatherings and stopped the distribution of bread. Still the rebellion grew in strength and eventually the people turned on the pharaoh and chose to worship a new God. They were told they were the chosen Israelites and had been wrongfully enslaved.

I knew that inside the pharaoh's heart and mind evil resided. Lust, power, and the whispers of the devil drove him to pour his hatred onto the people. He treated them as slaves which wore them down physically, but he never broke the will. Their minds remained strong.

Weeks passed and the pharaoh's resentment grew.

God's word touched the leader, Moses, and his brother. They proclaimed to be His messengers. They told everyone to trust them and God, as He would lead them out of their life of slavery.

Over the months, more angels descended upon the land, remaining invisible, keen to watch the battle unfolding between Pharaoh and the leader. Angels hadn't seen war in eons. Not since the time the angels first fell from the heavens.

I listened when God spoke to the leader's brother and foretold the first of ten plagues designed to free the slaves. I prepared myself for the coming destruction, while continuing to hope the humans would survive. Should they place their trust in the man who had God's ear, they would be fine.

The people flocked to the river to witness the brother of the leader using his fishing rod to defile the water. He turned it red. The fish died and the river smelled of death. The people then had no drinkable or usable water. The first plague had come.

The Pharaoh's magicians replicated the plague, claiming that high and low tides occurred monthly when the water resembled blood. They claimed the Egyptian god Khnum, the guardian of the Nile; Hapi the spirit of the Nile; and Osiris, the god of the underworld were insulted by this false plague.

The Pharaoh refused to listen to the leader's demands to release the Israelites.

Even after plagues of frogs, gnats, and flies spread across the land, the Pharaoh would not let the people leave.

I watched the little girl who I came to know as Rahabi, rally her kinsmen.

Livestock died, a plague of hail pounded the land, and then locusts covered the skies.

The Pharaoh still would not back down.

Then the plague of darkness fell.

Rahabi became the beacon of light; hope for the people.

I believed the lack of sun or moon for days would force the Pharaoh to change his mind, but it didn't. The devil had taken hold of Pharaoh's mind. I felt his evil spread across the land. I didn't realize that the devil controlling the Pharaoh was the original fallen angel, Sammael.

"I have a new plan," the Pharaoh's top adviser announced. "This that will ensure your subjects to return to their work."

"Speak, and let me hear," the Pharaoh said.

"Your people must be overcome by grief for their own family members." The advisor waved his hand across the pharaoh's face. He didn't blink for a long time. Then I watched as darkness swept through his body. "Kill all the females under the age of five."

This was a ploy for Sammael to stop the girl from the prophecy living to eighteen. We would have to be diligent and aware of our surroundings, now that I knew Sammael was involved. The Archangels had locked him in a blessed cage when they defeated him centuries ago, so someone else must be doing his bidding. That or else he was so powerful he could manipulate people from his prison.

One night while the land was still bathed in darkness, a guard entered the Rahabi's hut and swung his sword across her neck. Though I admired her, I couldn't stop her death. In my heart, I knew she wasn't the girl in the prophecy, we were not to intervene in any girls' life, unless there was a sliver of a chance she was the one whom we searched for. Still, her death weighed heavily on my mind and heart.

During the time spent watching her bake bread with her mom daily and following her to the river to wash clothes I had created a connection with her. I remembered the lone curl she constantly fiddled with because it wouldn't lay in the same direction as the others, and how her right eye had more tan speckles than the left.

I didn't know if I could continue to guard humans only to sit hopelessly by and watch them die at the hands of this evil spreading across the Earth. I was created to protect humans. That was why I was a Guardian angel and not a Choir angel.

As the people grieved and the girl's family mourned, it became clear I couldn't stand by and do nothing while evil continued to drain the good from these humans. I was unable to step in and save the humans from death, but I was able to do something. These humans must continue to fight for their freedom and stand against their oppressor.

Then the tenth plague was upon us.

Through the leader of the people, God declared the death of firstborns to people and cattle. He assigned a Guardian angel to each Israelite's family that would be spared. I stood in the company of a family as God's wrath swept the area. The door of each hut was marked with lamb's blood and an invisible angel's mark.

The next day, a deep grief encompassed the Pharaoh as his son was killed. He then finally allowed the people to leave.

It had taken ten brutal plagues from God to win the battle against the devil who whispered into Pharaoh's ear.

From that day forward, I remained resilient and watchful. Sammael had proven he would do unspeakable things to turn people against God. I now understood the depths of both their actions. The devil would stop at nothing to destroy the child who would prevent his release from prison to halt Armageddon.

Three

That first child's death made me rethink my task. I thought I knew what I'd gotten myself into when I raised my hand. My assignment to watch, listen, and protect was far harder than I could ever imagined. The girl's death changed me somehow and hardened my heart. I didn't want to do this anymore and that was what took me back to Heaven.

When I arrived in Heaven there were no other angels around. I was thankful for the solitude. Then the hushed melody from the choir of angels soothed my mind. I hovered for a long time, soaking in the warmth and letting it feed my soul.

I was home.

I wasn't sure how much time had passed. Did I even want to know? Probably not. I didn't want to be around anyone. I didn't want to speak to any other angels. Whatever they had to say, wouldn't change my mind, and it wouldn't bring the girl back. I had never attempted to search for her soul. I had contemplated it many times, but always I thought better of it. I wanted her soul to remain at peace.

My lieutenants checked in with me a few times after I arrived back in Heaven, but that didn't provide me with the amount of time that was passing on Earth. The only way I'd know was to return there. And I wasn't about to do that.

As time passed I grew restless. The time came when I had finally mustered the courage to seek out Michael. I didn't have to look far.

"Am I disturbing you?" a voice asked. "If you'd rather remain alone, I understand."

I whirled to confirm who had spoken and saw no one, but knew who belonged to that voice.

"No, Michael. I would welcome any advice you can give."

He appeared next to me, his wings invisible.

He patted my shoulder. "My first experience with evil and death still haunts me. It pained me to strike against my own brethren in the Battle of the Fallen, so I know exactly what you're going through. I'm pleased to see you again. It's been a while."

"I couldn't remain on Earth any longer. I had to leave" I hung my head low so Michael wouldn't see my eyes. "I'm not sure I'm cut out for this mission."

"And it's because you feel that way, I know you are. If what you saw hadn't affected you, I'd be worried. You're a gentle soul, Kieran, and one of the finest Guardian angels."

"My heart can't take feeling the human's pain and knowing I can't do anything about it. I'm powerless to halt the spread of evil, and unable to prevent Sammael from harming the humans."

"While that is true, I'm only hearing negative thoughts from you. You must focus on what you *can* do, which is to be there for the humans. They are a resilient species. Most have good intentions and their hearts are in the right place. It's those who flounder and become lost that we must help and steer them from the path that leads to darkness."

I took a deep breath. "Will you tell me about the Battle of the Fallen? If it's too painful to share . . . I'm sorry. That's private. I should never have asked—"

"Nonsense. You can ask me anything. I am your mentor. If I don't share my experiences, you won't learn from my mistakes."

Michael placed an arm around my shoulders and we started walking down a path through of clouds. "After Earth was created, most angels were happy with their existence. A few were not; they wanted more. So He created the humans. The angels who felt that they needed a different path took the responsibility to watch over the newly created man. The angels were intrigued by this species who lived such short lives, when we live forever. But soon He took more notice of his new children and a few angels grew to hate them. It was a new emotion, as our hearts had only ever been filled with pureness. Luciel—"

"The Seraph angel?" I asked.

"Yes. Luciel led the charge against Him and all the peaceful angels. As head Archangel for the Council, I was charged with stopping the rebellion. But Luciel was strong and convincing. He had swayed many angels to stand by his side and fight with him. It pained me to order the strike against him as we were inseparable for many eons. He was the closest I had to what humans call a best friend."

"Aren't all angels supposed to be our best friends?"

"Some have a greater pull. It's hard to explain if you've never felt it. It's like we were a part of each other. I would have laid down my existence for Luciel."

I nodded, even though I didn't understand. No other angel in Heaven shared that bond with me.

"The sides were drawn, and we needed to take up arms. Luciel was contaminating Heaven with ugly thoughts. He wanted the humans gone and was about to take all of his followers to annihilate them. I had just finished gathering my team when I learned of his plan. We met on the battlefield in the skies."

Michael stopped, looked around and then sat on a cloud in the shape of a bench.

"We don't talk much about the Battle of the Fallen because not many of us who witnessed it are left," he continued. "And those who did, don't want to be plagued with those harsh memories."

I wiped a tear from my eye. The way Michael had told the story—my own imagination filled in the gaps. My soul ached for the angels on both sides. Many angels' souls were snuffed out of existence. And that should never happen.

"How did you stop Luciel?" I asked.

"Before I answer that, let me back up a bit. The battle was not going to plan. Our side thought we could reason with Luciel, but he had different ideas. He struck first, killing angels. That's when we realized that not only did he truly believe in what he told his followers, but that he would do anything to get what he wanted. Even kill his own brethren.

"I called all the Archangels to battle. For a time, we were winning and halted their descent to Earth. But then Luciel did something unexpected. Until that point, he had stayed clear of me and only fought other angels. He confronted me. We came face to face and were equally matched."

"You say that like he's still alive."

"He is. Very much so. You know him as Sammael. He took that name when we locked him in the cage and proclaimed his revenge."

"How did he get there?"

"I drew my sword against him and we fought. We parried for a long time. Neither of us able to gain the upper hand. I was unaware what else was going on during the battle as my mind was focused solely on him. I was oblivious to the fact the Seraph angels had joined in the battle until I felt the presence of Grace, the lead Seraph angel. She assisted me. She used her Seraph Sword to strike Luciel's wing. He screamed, and was clearly in unimaginable pain which made him falter. I had no idea their swords could do that kind of damage. The Seraph angels don't come out often, so we don't know much about their powers. The other Seraph angels descended around him, pointing their swords at his throat. His followers stopped fighting when they saw he had been captured. More Archangels surrounded him. They each plucked a feather from Luciel's black wings, leaving him with only a single white one remaining. Grace molded the black feathers into the holy metal of Luciel's own sword, and infused it with Angel Light."

"So Luciel, I mean Sammael, doesn't have wings?"

"Yes and no. When the Angel Light took hold of Luciel,

it created a sphere-like prison made of himself. Because the Light came from Grace herself, he was unable to escape. The Archangels banished him to a realm lower than Earth to carry out his sentence, which I took him to. Luciel used the 'el' from his name and created the name for his new residence: Hell.

"But there is always a loophole to everything. He couldn't stay locked forever. Eventually he *could* be let out. With that lone feather, he would regenerate his wings over time, but not enough to allow him to escape. And that is where the prophecy is foretold.

Glory!
Babe born.
First and last.
Heaven and unto Earth.
Receives the highest in jubilation.
Enlightens will unite, they shall band.
Triumph be if darkness is driven back.
Help found who love, the world will stand.

"Hope, Kieran, is a wonderful emotion. For your next charge, you should walk in their shoes to understand this," Michael said. "Hope is a valuable thing. For some, it's all they have. It's all we had before, during, and after the Battle, and we continue to carry that hope with us."

I nodded.

"Become an Ordinary. Lose the wings. You'll still retain all of your angelic powers. You can manipulate your appearance if you choose, but you'll will need a believable back story when you appear to her. I'll leave you to determine that. I'm sure you can come up with the rest."

Then Michael disappeared, leaving me to my solitude once again.

"I'll always be here to guide you. Remember that, Kieran." Michael's voice echoed in my mind.

I pondered what he had said. It was true that I had been dwelling on the negative when I should have been concentrating on ways to help the Ordinaries.

Resolved, I departed Heaven to search for my next charge.

Four

Sixteen Hundred Sixty-Six: Spring

London, England

"Kieran, you need to come to London." The voice of one of my Lieutenants, Harper, rang through my mind.

"What's happening?" I responded.

"It's better if you see for yourself."

Horses, carts, and houses lined the many cobblestoned streets. I remained behind a small cottage and watched the humans go about their business. Listening to unrecognizable words, I took note of what they wore, then imagined myself in something similar and exchanged my light blue, gauzy gown for a simple tan smock and brown cloak, as well as little brown slippers. My wings disappeared and I made myself visible, but kept my twenty-something appearance, as I walked among them.

"Harper, where are you?"

"We're in a warehouse at the edge of town."

After I arrived, we watched two females enter the building. Five male Ordinaries stood inside. I immediately made myself invisible.

"We've been following the short female who just entered."

I inspected the humans standing inside the building. They were not humans though; they were demons. Their glowing red eyes were the first things to give them away. Then I looked deeper and it became obvious what they were. Under their pale human-like skin, their mangled bodies were red skinned and oozed black pus. I'd never seen anything like them. Their souls, marked in black, still pumped blood, the telltale sign that they were once human.

"I don't understand, Harper."

"Just wait, Kieran. You'll see."

In the next moment, the smaller of the two females sprinted straight into a group of three demons. She caught one by surprise and slashed his chest in half. I watched, stunned. The other two demons scrambled into a defensive stance as her muscular arms and legs whirled, connecting with their stomachs, heads, and backs. She was amazing to watch. And something about her made me pause. She wasn't really an Ordinary; she was something else.

"They call her Jessa," Harper said.

Her tall companion twisted her hand and she sent both her demons flying backwards against the wall. Their bodies crumpled to the floor. A few seconds later, one rose to his feet and shook his head. He charged at her.

An energized shimmer filled the air. Green light swirled around her. I knew immediately she wasn't an Ordinary, either.

But something else was happening.

A wind vortex then slammed into the standing demon. His body crashed alongside a support beam, and I heard an undeniable crack from his back.

The other demon howled and ran at her, slashing a knife in the air. She redirected the wind and blew his weapon from his hands, rendering him useless, then somehow she threw a couple of handfuls of pebbles at his feet. He slid, lost his balance, and fell backward, cracking his skull on the stone floor. Like his friend, he would not get up again.

"That was awesome!" Jessa, the shorter female exclaimed. "If I'd known you could do all that, I wouldn't have had you do the Mind Walk."

"What is she talking about?" I asked.

"The little one can read minds," Harper said.

Jessa bent over the demon with the broken back and sliced smoothly through his jugular. "He doesn't need to be in pain," she explained to her friend. "Father says to end the DKs quickly."

"DKs?" I questioned.

"Demon Knights."

"What's the other one's name?"

"Sidelle."

What a unique name. I tested her name on my lips: Sidelle.

Jessa then grinned and said over her shoulder to Sidelle, "I think you're going to be our new favorite weapon."

I watched an incredible smile spread across Sidelle's face. It warmed my heart. I tossed around ideas as to what those two females could be. Neither was human, but they looked like it. Then again, I could pass for an Ordinary. Maybe they had some sort of power.

They weren't angels, though.

"Boss?" Nishan asked. *"Now you know why we called you here."*

"Yes. Show yourself, please," I instructed them.

Both materialized in gauzy robes, but kept their wings hidden.

"I'm sure you have many questions," Harper said. "We

did too when we first came to the city." He looked at his partner. "We had no idea . . . about . . ."

"About what?"

"Werewolves and fairies," Nishan said. "London is protected by a wolf pack. They fight the demons and keep the Ordinaries safe, for the most part. But then a new girl started hanging around." He looked around, probably to make sure we were still alone, then said, "She's a Summer Fairy."

"So tell me all you know about them and the demons."

"Gage Venator is the Alpha, his daughter, Jessa, who we just watched best three demons is his Beta," Nishan said. "The London Pack is comprised of about twenty werewolves. They call themselves Naturals because they live longer lives than an Ordinary, about twice as long, in fact. Some of the younger members turn on the night of a full moon, but the older ones can control it more.

"They can block some of the fairy's glamour. Glamour is like magic. Sidelle can manipulate the weather, her appearance, and can hear thoughts of the humans, but not the wolves. We're not sure if she can't or if they won't let her.

"Demon Knights are responsible for causing most of the so-called 'manmade' destruction in the world, like the Holy Wars," Harper said. "When they are killed on Earth their bodies disintegrate, but we don't know where they go. We think all Knights are susceptible to human weaknesses.

"Marquises Demons are mid-level demons typically found in small groups. They are the fighters of Hell. They are ruthless and brutal, and they're also expert swordsmen. They start 'natural disasters,' like floods, erupting volcanoes, and fires. We've heard of the pack talking about someone the demons call the Prince, but they don't have any information on him. They've started calling Sammael 'the king.' And interesting enough, the demons know it was the Seraph angels who locked the devil in the cage when he fell from Heaven after the Battle of the Fallen."

"I see." My head turned toward the path the two young women left. "I'll let Michael know about them. Have you found the babe?"

"No," Harper said. "We thought there was something strange about the one called Jessa. That's why we followed her, but then figured out what she actually was."

"Okay. Keep watching both of them. I'll be back as soon as I can. I want to observe them for a while."

"Yes, boss," both said in unison.

Following my instructions, they disappeared. I never knew angels lived among fairies, or of the existence of werewolves. Sure, I heard rumors of other "beings." If this was a shock for me, I wondered what Michael would say about it.

To watch the tall, black-haired beauty fight and easily

take down two demons with just a flick of her wrist was amazing to witness. She moved with grace that could easily be mistaken for an angel. The feeling that washed through me when her Glamour came to her call was awe inspiring. My own wings fluttered as I felt Earth's energy being disturbed. Then to see Sidelle use her magic and manipulate it . . . I came to respect the fairy, even though I didn't know her.

Jessa—the werewolf—her fighting skills could put to shame even the Nephilim. I'd seen some of the half-angels before. With their enhanced human abilities of speed, strength, and vision; that's how they became Heaven's warriors. In my mind's eye, I reenacted the battle scene, their movements, and all I'd just learned about them.

I didn't hesitate any longer. Night had fallen and I didn't need to worry about being seen. My golden wings appeared and then I extended them as they carried me toward the heavens.

Instead of basking in the glow of Heaven's light, I sought out Michael.

He appeared instantly. "Kieran, I've been expecting you. I assume you have many questions for me."

"Yes. Yes, I do." My wings vanished while we floated in the clouds. Michael's version of Heaven morphed into a white sandy beach. "Did you know about them?" I didn't elaborate.

"Yes." He looked at me. "I recruited Sidelle a long time

ago. She's had a difficult time in Fairyland, her home. Someone broke her heart and she needed a change. I knew this task would do her well."

"You knew about the werewolves, too?"

"Of course."

"And you didn't tell me about them? I would have thought it'd be something to share. That I would need to know about them . . . and the demons."

"But you know about them now?" We stopped at the tree line. Michael caressed a small purple flower from the branches that hung low near our heads.

"Yes, from Nishan and Harper."

"Would you have believed me if I would've told you?"

"Of course."

After the row of trees, the area opened up. We floated across a river. I looked down. It was so clear that I couldn't tell if it was real or not. The only sound was a small gurgling noise.

"Maybe. Kieran, sometimes there are things you need to see with your own eyes."

"Where do they come from?"

"Which?"

"Both."

"Fairies have existed as long as the angels. They just are. They live in a realm called Fairyland, which is divided into now five sections: Summer, Winter, two In-between territories, and the Mist. Summer and Winter are ruled by royalty figures. King Oberon rules Summer and Queen Mab rules Winter. No one rules the Mist."

"Why do you say 'now five sections'? Was that not always the case?"

"No. There used to be Summer, Winter and the Mist."

"So then how did the In-between territories come about? And who rules there?"

"Something happened many centuries ago that I don't have much information on. The Fairies are being tight-lipped about it. I don't even know if they understand it. So no one rules the In-between, as far as I know . . . yet."

"Does anyone live in the Mist? It seems ominous."

"It's where the non-Glamour fairies live, and other 'things.' Their powers derive from Earth."

I nodded, keeping up.

"The werewolves were created by the angels," Michael continued. "Angel Light was bestowed upon them eons ago. We mixed our essence with those of humans, giving them agility and longer lifespans. And in return, they'd be our eyes on Earth. Back then there were few demons roaming, but enough to cause concern for the Council."

As I listened, the scenery changed again. My hand swept across the waist-high bright green grass, feeling the soft prickles against my fingers.

"The Council sought out worthy families. We gave our Light to the head of a family on each continent, and where the population was the densest."

"Why have them change forms with the moon?"

"Unfortunate ramification of not enough Angel Light. Their bodies couldn't handle it. But we got it right when we created the Nephilim."

"I thought Nephilim were created by a fallen angel and human."

"They technically are. But if angels get to them when they are newly created and infuse a little bit more of Angel Light into them, they'll work for good and not become a Marquises Demon."

"Thank you for the information. I understand a little more. I don't think I would have fully understood you if you told me this first. My experience has been so limited with humans in general. I never would have thought about the existence of other 'beings.'"

"Good. I'll take my leave so you can go back to Earth."

I was dismissed.

Five

My Angel Light cast an intense yellow circle on the ground, cutting through the thick fog of London. There was a dark gloom that lingered around my heart the moment I entered Earth's realm.

I immediately sought out Sidelle.

Battle cries, screams, and wailing horns came from all directions. Smoke filled the air, not fog.

I made my way toward the howling werewolves. They were created by Angel Light, so I could find them easily. Each blinked like a star in my mind.

I found Jessa first. She fought against a few DKs, but her fairy partner wasn't to be found. Sure both could get by, they had been before I came along, but a nagging pulled me toward wanting to protect them—Sidelle. Two were better than one, right?

Appearing before Jessa, I drew my sword and sliced one of her opponents.

"Thanks! I don't know how many of them came through the veil last night." She wasn't startled to see me. "Go find and help Sidelle. I think she's up a few streets," she screamed. "I can handle these!"

I hesitated.

"*Go!*"

Nodding my head, I disappeared. *It didn't faze her that I'm an angel.* I was about to reappear when I felt the earth shake, like an earthquake tremor. Something wasn't right. I was suspended in mid-air and felt . . . off. Fear blanketed my body and I knew I had to find her.

It didn't take me long to lock on Sidelle's location. She stood surrounded by a group of demons. Of course she was in the thick of it.

I stopped a few moments to admire her. The harsh words spewing at the demons from her soft lips. She taunted them, forcing them to strike her first so she could unleash the fury she tried to hide. All her pain from whatever had happened to her in Fairyland, waiting to be released.

I was here to help, not stare at her.

"Why don't you try taking on someone your own size?" I asked the black-hooded creatures, standing with my golden wings wrapped around my body and my silver sword extended. I turned to Sidelle. "I heard you needed some help."

"You heard wrong," she said, slightly annoyed, her sword's tip now aimed at my chest. "I was just about to dispose of this rodent."

I chuckled. Her attitude stopped me in my tracks, not knowing for sure if she meant it. I assumed they were a front and all she really needed was a friend. Or love.

My Light faded the demon to a shade of gray, and then I froze him in place. The Marquises coughed helplessly.

"There are more where he came from." I glanced around. "We should team up. My Light won't hold him forever."

She lowered her sword. "I already have a partner."

Always being the tough one.

"Jessa?" I confirmed. "Yeah, she sent me to you."

She gave a mock curtsy, then spun around to face the demon. "Fine. If it'll get you off my case, then by all means, have at it."

A few seconds later, the Marquises Demon became unfrozen and back to full strength. His face scrunched, and he huffed. His hands formed a triangle, and he puffed a breath into it like he was cold. As if on cue, four more Marqs rose like the dead from the ground.

Sidelle gathered her Glamour and shot it directly at the demon, but it had no effect. It sailed through him and hit a tree, spraying green light all over the trunk, fizzling like water droplets. She uprooted the tree and used the branches to grab the demon around the waist. While the tree held him steady, her sword sliced through the neck. The creature's head rolled off . . . and a few seconds later it grew back.

I had a difficult time dealing with all the newcomers. At this rate, we would be overrun. We'd have to flee if reinforcements didn't arrive soon. I didn't have much time to watch Sidelle fight, but I caught a few glimpses. Her graceful movements reminded me of a well-rehearsed dance. The blackness of her hair swallowed me whole.

A lone howl filled the night's air, and pounding footsteps sounded from far away, growing louder with each step. Help was on its way. Multiple howls answered the first, and I knew the pack was closing in.

But so were more Marquises Demons. They had appeared from all directions.

The screams of men and women swelled, and I was even more determined to win the fight. We had to keep the Ordinaries safe; they couldn't fight this battle. I ran toward their cries.

"We need to retreat!" I yelled to Sidelle.

"There is no backing down," she screamed back.

"I know but those humans—"

"Yeah, okay."

We turned the corner, and came face to face with a

pack of DKs. At least my Light worked on these demons. I blasted them with pure golden light as my fairy partner blew through their ranks like a machine, cutting, slicing, and beheading. I never looked back to check on Sidelle again.

The Ordinaries' screams pushed me on, and Sidelle ran to my side. We had a break in the fight. *I must leave you for a bit so I can see the landscape,* I told Sidelle in her mind. Before she could respond, I wrapped my wings around myself and spun—then I shot like a cannon into the sky unfurling my golden feathers.

"Michael, I need your help! Bring any and all Archangels you can. Earth is being overrun with demons."

I entered the upper skies, the clouds parted, and a mass of multi-colored, winged angels descended.

"Kieran, we are here," Michael's voice responded. *"Move the humans to safety and leave the Marquises to us."*

The Archangels flew to the streets, some gathered the Ordinaries and moved them off to the side while others took up their swords and joined the battle.

I dropped back to the ground. "I brought reinforcements."

"So I see," Sidelle acknowledged.

I smirked. Her tough exterior started peeling away.

"The Archangels will take on the Marquises," I said. "You and I are to corral the Ordinaries and bring them to a safe place, or to anywhere outside the direct battlefronts.

If we run into the Marqs, do the best you can, but keep moving. The pack will go where it's needed."

"Who made you the boss?" She raised one sardonic brow. "Have you seen Jessa? I need to make sure she's okay."

"Don't worry about her. She can take care of herself. She's with her pack." I gestured toward the street. "Look, there's a family trapped between the houses."

Since Sidelle passed as a normal-looking human, I made myself visible to assist her. We herded the Ordinaries back into one of the homes, and Sidelle swept for hiding demons. Finally, we could rest and mentally regroup.

"Who are you, anyway?" she asked. "And are you always so bossy?"

"I'm Kieran. And yes. So everyone tells me. It's nice to finally meet you, Sidelle."

"You know of me?"

"Michael told me about you." I didn't think I should tell her that I've been watching her for a while.

"The Archangel?"

"The one and the only."

She walked toward the door, and I followed. "How do you know him?"

"I report to him," I said.

"What about them?" Sidelle pointed back into the house and at the Ordinaries. "Are we going to let them remember what they saw?"

I nodded. "For now." My chin jerked toward the street. "Don't worry about them. Let's get back out there. I'm sure there are more to save."

Six

Sixteen Hundred Sixty-Eight

Somewhere in Asia

I had to see Sidelle again.

My brief encounter with her wasn't cutting it. Something about her pulled at me. Maybe it was her snow-white skin calling to my soul and making me wonder what it would feel like to embrace her and feel her body cradled in my arms. Maybe it was her emerald-green eyes that showed the depths of her emotions, which she desperately tried to hide from everyone. Or maybe it was the brave front she gave through her quick, witty chatter.

Just thinking about her melodic voice emitting from those kissable lips made me pause. I wanted to feel those lips against mine.

Whoa.

I was an angel, and we didn't have those feelings. Did we? No. Well . . . maybe. I obviously felt something for her.

My heady emotions swirled around me. I liked having them. Of course, I didn't really understand what they meant. But I had to see her again.

When I closed my eyes and opened my angelic powers, I found her someplace in Asia. Her eternal soul shone bright green and was easy to spot in the midst of the humans.

Today she was training outdoors. There were no matts to soften falls, only trampled blades of grass. A smattering of trees outlined the area. Off in the distance, rolling rice paddies filled with workers dotted the horizon. She wore simple black, cotton pants and a tunic.

I guessed she probably didn't want anything to do with me so I remained invisible as my eyes watched her lithe body move with graceful movements.

She kicked, lashed, and hit her opponent with the ferocity that I never wanted to be the brunt of. Then taking on three or four master-level men at a time, she flawlessly escaped her captors and turned the stakes in a matter of moments.

She was a force, just like the wind power she created to defeat the demons. Never breaking into a sweat. Never stopping to catch her breath. Teams of martial artists battled against her and none going easy on her just because she was female.

I respected them for that. Sidelle could take anything thrown her way.

Maybe even me.

The sparring match continued for a few more minutes. Bodies lay on the ground, slow to rise. A few younger men held up their hands in defeat, calling it quits.

Sidelle cracked her neck, stretched out her legs, and shook her arms out. With a little bounce in her step, I knew she still wanted to fight more.

I looked around making sure that most everyone had left. In my mind I fashioned similar attire to match hers. I appeared, without my wings, in the shadow of the tree line.

"Still looking for someone who could take you?" I asked.

Her eyes turned instantly in my direction.

"It's you." She stepped toward me. "Couldn't get enough of me?"

"No, I couldn't." Her eyes widened a bit. Probably surprised I told her the truth. "So are we going to do this or not?" She scanned me from head to toe.

I felt her blush from where I stood.

"Fine, but don't complain when you can't fly later," she smirked.

But the gleam in her eyes said she wasn't going to go easy on me. I didn't think she would.

"No using Glamour." I marched forward into the clearing. "Swords or hand-to-hand?"

"Swords are for children." Her gaze ran down my body and her eyes softened a bit. "Don't use your powers, either."

I smiled, then nodded.

We circled each other, neither of us wanting to strike first. I was glad I had the short opportunity to watch her fight back in London and now a few moments ago in a new strange style. But being an angel did have its perks. Instantly, I knew all sorts of combatting skills.

Sidelle stepped forward, I retreated.

In a crouching position, she narrowed her eyes. Challenging me.

I advanced. Following her, never taking my eyes off her subtle movements. My feet stepped lightly on the ground getting closer with each pass. Stalking.

Finally, she swung at me with an open palm, going for my head. I easily dodged the hit. Her leg shot out in a sweeping motion, narrowly missing my feet.

I think she was testing me and my abilities.

Then she let it all out. Charging me, her arms and hands flew in all directions so fast. Striking me every so often. I went on the defensive, attempting to block her hits. She landed a few more good punches to my chin and stomach. My arms shielding my face, forgetting about her long legs.

But not for long.

Sidelle landed a kick that brought me to the ground. She didn't give me any time to stand. Her small fists flew to my head as I lay. Pounding fiercely with all her might. Using everything she had with precision blows. Her legs pinned my thighs.

Whoever taught her, did so very well.

I managed to catch her balled hand as it went near my check. I stopped her momentum and twisted my upper body. She now lay under me. I gazed into her round face and sucked in a breath. A small smile spread across on her lips. My eyes dropped to her mouth.

Feeling her warm body beneath mine. I closed my eyes, savoring the moment. Then I remembered we were supposed to be sparring. I moved off her. "Sorry."

She struck like a viper.

Pain shot though my chest when her elbow connected. I bent over, blinking away the fading stars.

"You're going easy on me," Sidelle hissed.

I shook my head and stood straight. The look on her face told me she was ready for whatever I inflicted. My arms and legs burst out with renewed energy. I was on the offensive, driving her back.

I flinched when my fist connected with her side. She let out a loud sigh. I froze in place. I didn't mean to hit her that hard.

Her breath deepened.

Round and round we went, each landing a few hits. Neither of us could best the other. If she continued, I wouldn't be able to fly just like she said. Was I letting her win on purpose?

No . . . maybe.

With renewed efforts, Sidelle ran and grabbed a sword. I blinked. Fine, we'll play it her way. I seized a broken rattan from a pile of discarded weapons left from her opponents.

We parried.

Sweat soaked my clothes. I didn't know how long we fought, but my body was tiring. My movements were slower than when I started. I noticed her strikes weren't as precise, either. She was fading, too.

We danced. Well, not really, but I'd like to think it was like a well-rehearsed routine.

I lowered my rattan to my side . . . in defeat. She won. Not that I would say that out loud.

I crumpled to the ground, catching my breath. Eventually I fell backwards feeling the cold dirt cooling off my body.

Sidelle dropped her sword and sat beside me. Her eyes lingered on my chest. She swallowed.

That was twice I caught her checking me out.

Clapping brought me out of my thoughts. I noticed the small crowd of bystanders who gathered to witness our fight. They departed since there was nothing else to see.

We stayed in that position for a long time.

Eventually we found ourselves alone. A light breeze blew across my face, drying my damp clothes.

Sidelle smiled, but it didn't reach her eyes.

I knew she created the wind. I felt her gather her Glamour around us and then noticed her dry and clean clothes.

I wanted to ask her so many things about being a fairy, what she was doing on this side of the earth, and most importantly whom she was running from.

But I held my tongue.

She would tell me if she wanted me to know. And she didn't know me. I barely knew her, let alone this new side of me. The part wanting to be around her.

"You're a good fighter," Sidelle said, breaking the silence. "For an angel." She winked.

"You're not bad yourself . . . for a fairy." I smiled.

She looked like she wanted to say more. Her eyes swirled with emotion like she was fighting inside her own head.

I reached for her and laced my fingers between hers. She looked down at me, then to our joined hands.

In that instant, something passed between us. A hum. I

didn't know if it was me or her doing it, but I could see her memories from what I thought was Fairyland.

Lush green landscape . . . clear water . . . a wooden row boat . . . and a dark-haired fairy dressed in shades of blue.

Sadness crept over me, and then a hint of anger.

Her fury from a long time ago. It still resonated deep in her soul. I saw it there. And that made me love her even more.

Sure I cared for her, but love?

Sidelle's eyes returned to my face. She sucked in a breath. Had she heard that thought of mine? No, that's not possible.

"Michael," we said at the same time. We both looked at each other and shook our heads.

"I'm on a secret mis—," Sidelle started.

"We're on the same mission?" I asked.

"I think we are."

"I haven't found her yet."

"Neither have I. So I've been passing the time learning skills."

"Not a bad idea."

I called my Angel Light and let it wash over her. My memories of seeing her the first time outside the warehouse, ready to take on three demons. Then as she drew on the Glamour and defeated them. And finally when I introduced myself to her in the midst of battle in London.

"Is that how you see me?" She blinked.

"Yes. You're beautiful." I ran my fingers down the side of her cheek. "The most beautiful being I've ever laid eyes on." Her skin was so soft, as velvety as one of my own feathers.

I propped myself up on my elbows.

A storm waged on Sidelle's face.

And then it cleared.

She closed the short distance between us by taking my face in her palms.

She smelled like a spring rain. I inhaled, deeply.

Then, she kissed me. It was hesitant at first. But a passion burned just below the surface.

I was in shock. My body finally caught up to my brain.

I was kissing Sidelle!

My arms wrapped around her lean body, pulling her closer.

A few moments later, she squirmed out of my hold.

Too soon for her. She still ached in her heart.

I sighed and stood, extending my hand to help her up. To my surprise, she placed her hand into mine and rose.

"That was fun . . . the sparring, too," she said. "We should do that again sometime."

I didn't know if she meant the kissing or fighting.

"You know. I wasn't expecting to see you ever." She dusted off her clothes. "How did you find me?"

"I can find anyone who I've met before. You're not hard

to locate."

She nodded and stepped away, sheathing her sword. "So tell me what happened in London after the fire."

"We had to wipe half of the city's occupants' minds so they didn't remember seeing angels, demons, and werewolves. After that, Michael with the help from other Archangels created the Void—a parallel place that lies between Earth and Heaven." I came to stand beside her, noticing for the first time how tall she was. She stood almost eye level to me. "The Void is a space where we can hide some of what goes on in our world to keep it away from the Ordinaries. Demons might not care who they hurt, but the angels' mission is to protect the humans. If we take our fights to the Void, it would raise fewer concerns and suspicions."

"That's good."

"Sidelle." She stood inches from my face and yet I could feel her pulling away. "I won't apologize for kissing you."

"I think it was me who kissed you first."

I nodded. "So it was."

"But I can't. Not yet." She dropped her voice. "I—"

"You don't have to explain. I saw it. I'm sorry he hurt you."

"Yeah, me, too. Please don't come after me. I need time." She hung her head, turned and walked away from me.

Sidelle never sought me out. I tried to give her space. She mourned someone. I never got her to say his name, but that didn't matter. I didn't want to know. It was because of him that she and I couldn't be together.

Well, Eternals from different Orders couldn't be together. So there's that. Tell that to my brain and heart.

As an angel, it was my nature to help, be supportive, and well, be a protector—a guardian. Not that she needed any of those things from me. She'd rip off my wings in a flash if she thought I considered her weak.

I saw her broken heart. Of course I kept tabs on her. She just didn't know I was there and if she did, she never said anything.

Seven

Sixteen Hundred Ninety-One: Winter

Province of Massachusetts Bay: Salem Village

Eventually I made my way to the west, the new land across the ocean. I planted myself in a growing town they called Salem Village. After the death of my first charge and the realization that werewolves and fairies lived among us, I needed a change. And maybe I was running a bit, too.

I couldn't get Sidelle out of my mind.

The softness of her lips.

The firm muscles of her body. How they flexed and bent as she fought.

All was quiet from my lieutenants. They hadn't seen

any demons they couldn't handle themselves. Plus, they didn't come across the girl we had been searching for. It was a good thing some of us were doing our jobs.

Then another young lady entered into my life. She made me rethink my whole philosophy on things. I was not ready for her to become a part of my existence.

Elizabeth.

She had been born years earlier than my arrival to the colonies. It had never dawned on me to look for an almost grown adult—that she could be the one we sought.

I came across a shoe shop, which had reminded me of Sidelle. Thoughts of her popped into my head over the strangest things. At times, I missed her. Maybe it was her snippy attitude. Yes, we fought, but I knew it was a front. And that kiss . . .

A young lady passed me on the cobblestone path, dressed in a solid black dress. Her head was covered by a black bonnet. She walked slowly, sniffling as she strolled by.

But when I brushed past, her green eyes locked with mine. I knew she couldn't see me. Or could she? There was no doubt in my mind I was invisible. Over the centuries I had learned some other angelic powers: to disguise smells, sounds, and touch. As I kept walking from her, my wings told me she still watched my retreating back. She held her keen gaze on me, as if she did see right into my soul. My wings told me she still watched my retreating back. I looked over my shoulder and I caught her.

She smiled.

A chill went through my wings, but it wasn't because I felt an evil being. No. Somehow, I sensed she didn't mean harm to me. Maybe there were other beings in the world like her. She was something else. Since I had met fairies and werewolves before, I knew their signatures and what made them different from the Ordinaries.

She intrigued me.

I changed directions and followed her. She wound her away around the streets. People parted as she walked by. Every now and then, she'd glance over her shoulder as if she knew I was trailing her. A small smile played on her lips.

Still not feeling any maliciousness, I continued to shadow her until she stopped in front of a brown, brick house. With one last look back, she opened the door and stood waiting for me to pass through. She watched me as I glided by. And then she reached out to touch my bare shoulder.

It sent shivers down my spine and through my wings.

I wasn't ready to reveal myself, even when she confirmed that she could see me.

Two other women were in the house, already seated on the couch in the living room. Both their heads glanced up when I entered. It was the strangest feeling to know that all three women knew I was there.

"Elizabeth," the older looking woman said. "You've made it. I'm glad you were able to speak with us even though you are in mourning." She rose and gave Elizabeth a light kiss on the cheek. "Welcome."

"Thank you for inviting me, Jane," Elizabeth said. "This is all new to me, so I'm glad you are allowing me to observe first."

"Of course," the other lady said. "We don't want to pressure you. There is a certain amount of trust we must form . . . since—" She looked around the room. "This is an illegal gathering."

Oh, what had I gotten myself into?

"Sarah, if you wouldn't mind?" Jane asked.

Sarah nodded and the lights flickered out with a breeze that even I felt. It blew by me like an invisible ghost circling the room, extinguishing each wall sconce. Heavy curtains blocked any remnants of the late afternoon sun. The room was left in total darkness.

The one they called Jane seemed to be the leader of the trio. She spoke, barely above a whisper, as the air around her fizzled. Her arms rose high above her head, repeating the same garbled phrase. I floated toward her to listen.

As clear as I could hear she said, "I call on the earth to hear my wishes." She stood. "I call on the earth to show me what's not seen."

The air felt electrically charged.

"I call on the earth to hear my wishes," Sarah said. "I call on the earth to show me what's not seen."

Jane and Sarah joined hands and continued to chant the same lines. With their other hands, they offered an invitation to Elizabeth. She looked at each woman and then joined the circle, saying the same sentences.

My wings pulsed.

I checked everyone's aura again, just to make sure they weren't fairies. Negative. They were, in fact, humans. But then something strange happened.

The shield I kept around my body faded. My wings pulsed violently and then appeared without my doing. A slight gasp escaped my lips. I could feel my body pulling in two directions: one to remain unseen and the other to appear before these women.

As they chanted, I couldn't stop it. I couldn't hold it back any longer.

Their eyes opened and locked onto mine.

I now stood in the center of the circle, no longer invisible.

My mouth dropped open and my eyes widened, but the women didn't notice. They stared at my golden wings, which expanded the length of the small room. Or possibly at my bare chest. Thinking I should cover my half-naked body, I imagined myself in a white tunic and suddenly I was dressed.

The chanting ceased. The candles in the room lit.

"Welcome, Angel," Jane said. "We don't mean you harm." She let go of Elizabeth's hand. "I wanted to show our newcomer what we do, and I knew you came in with her. I'm sorry if we outted you, but I couldn't think of anything else that would make Elizabeth believe we have magical abilities."

I looked into the eyes of each woman. Jane held mine, but the other two lowered theirs. I forced my Angel Light around me. Not that I wanted them scared, but more so that they knew I was a force to reckon with.

Adjusting my wings so they didn't take up the room, I stepped toward Jane. I extended my hand to hers. She grasped it tightly, then pulled me into a hug.

In that moment I knew without a doubt that these women were not cruel beings. If they were, could they stand to be in the presence of an angel so pure? So full of love?

"Peace be with you," I said.

"And also with you," Sarah responded. "You probably know who we are, but do you have a name? Or something that the others call you?"

"I am Kieran."

"What kind of angel are you?" Elizabeth asked.

"A Guardian."

"Oh, are you tasked with watching over one of us? Is that why you were following me?"

"No."

"A man . . . an angel of few words," Jane said. "Well, you know what I mean. We welcome you to the Salem Coven. If you're not here to watch over us, then why were you trailing Elizabeth?"

"I'm trying to find someone."

"Can't you use your angelic powers?" Elizabeth asked.

"It doesn't work like that." I shook my head.

"Maybe we can help you?" Sarah asked.

I declined the offer.

"You're here because?" Jane asked me.

"I wanted to understand what you are." I slowly approached the couch, gesturing for them all to sit.

"We are the Witches of Salem."

"How many are there of you?" The three of them sat together on the sofa, while I chose the chair.

"Now, now. We can't tell you that and reveal how strong we are."

"Then I'll assume you have many in your coven. Is that why I can't get a read on you? Or why I can't read your minds?"

"You can do that?" Jane asked.

"Yes. I'm supposed to hear your thoughts and prayers. But from you three, I don't hear anything. Your minds are in total silence." It reminded me of Sidelle's powers, of how she could block me probing her thoughts. "I know you're not normal humans. That much I do know."

"You are correct. We are not." Jane nodded. "Trust is a

two-way street, though. You show us what you can do and we'll show you the witch's power. But for now, Kieran, let's get to know each other. Where will you be staying? Will you need a place to rest? I'll offer you one of my spare rooms so you can keep up appearances while you're in town."

"That is nice of you to think of. Thank you."

"This way you can still come and go as you wish."

"I usually do, yes. I don't require a roof over my head, so to speak. I don't need food to sustain myself, nor sleep. I just am. I shall be in and out of the house during the night, but you'll know when I'm here or not. If you need me, just call my name and I'll be there." I rose. "I haven't been on this side of Earth so I have to learn many things."

"All right." Jane stood and placed a warm hand on my shoulder. "But please remember to use caution outside of these walls. We're not always the most welcomed, and people love to demean the things they don't understand. Don't judge by what you hear from others."

"I do not feel you to be malicious in nature. I'll take my leave so you can resume your meeting."

With a nod to the ladies, I disappeared.

Eight

I floated around the town of Salem, in a colony they called Massachusetts.

The city's cobblestone roads, the layout, the smells—it all reminded me of London, and of course, that in turn, reminded me of Sidelle. What was it about her that I was drawn to? I only met her for a twitch in time since both of us lived forever, yet she left such an impact on my life.

A group of bystanders caught my attention in a small park on Washington Square.

There in the middle was a raised platform with people standing a top of it in lavish attire. One man dressed in fine clothes with a golden crown on his head sat in an ornate chair. On his side, a female draped across his arm in an elegant green gown. A matching crown on her head.

Others jested, making people laugh. While more stood in winged clothes.

I scrunched my face. A blatant disrespect and a mockery of the angels. And of Him.

As I soared toward them about to give them a piece of my mind, the man spoke in a different language. It was a version of English I had heard many centuries ago. I stopped before I could do anything harsh.

Not revealing myself, I listened to the words.

"The king doth keep his revels here to-night," the jester said. "Take heed the queen come not within his sight. For Oberon is passing fell and wrath, because that she as her attendant hath. A lovely boy, stolen from an Indian king. She never had so sweet a changeling; and jealous Oberon would have the child Knight of his train, to trace the forests wild; but she perforce withholds the loved boy, crowns him with flowers, and makes him all her joy . . ."

A winged human responded, "Either I mistake your shape and making quite, Or else you are that shrewd and knavish sprite. Called Robin Goodfellow . . ."

The wings, the stage setting, the characters reminded me of Fairyland. Could they be speaking of *the* King Oberon of Summer? I knew the playwright, William Shakespeare, when he wrote the story back in 1595. Someone, and my guess was Sidelle, had whispered in his ear the storyline.

Had she given William his inspiration for *A Midsummer*

Night's Dream?

More onlookers convened around the open-air stage as the main characters continued reciting lines. I watched as fairies ran across the stage in their version of flying. So humans must know of fairies, or at least they understood that they were made-up characters. How little did they realize that the whole story was true. Except that the changeling in the play was not a boy, but a girl—Sidelle.

That gave me pause.

I had heard rumblings in Europe about humans with fairy-like abilities, but I didn't pay attention to the rumors. I thought I knew that no human possessed magic, even elemental magical qualities. Someone named those groups of people witches. And here I had seen firsthand a little of that magic.

The next day, I stopped in front of Elizabeth's bungalow. She wasn't hard to find in the sea of human auras. Hers shone brighter. Like the north star in the sky; I couldn't stay away from her.

I watched as she went about her daily routine: washing clothes and bed linens, cooking and cleaning her house. Every so often she brushed stray tears from her face. She never acknowledged my presence, but she knew I was there.

Then she let me see why she was alone. She opened

her mind to me and recalled the day that made her so sad.

She had lost her husband a few weeks ago in a terrible accident. At the last minute, Elizabeth had changed her mind to attend a party, feeling sick that night. Her husband left her at their house. The next morning when he hadn't returned, Elizabeth woke and went looking for him. Her first stop was the residence of the host of the party. They had told her that her husband never arrived.

She followed the road she thought the carriage would take, where she came upon the accident.

I knew instantly that something was amiss when I saw the image. No earthly being could create the scene. The horse's reins hung in the shape of an imaginary horse. The black carriage lay in ruins. The upturned wheels still spun. Two bodies were wedged under the splintered door.

An evil presence still lingered in the air.

Dried blood seeped from the mouth of one of the men. The other's neck bent at an odd angle. Both had been dead for a long time.

Elizabeth ran to the man whose neck was broken. She tried lifting the door away from his body, but it was heavy. It was too late to save him anyway. She flung herself onto the rain-soaked ground, not caring she'd get dirty.

Tears fell from her face. A mournful wail flowed from her, causing bystanders to notice.

How others couldn't see the broken carriage, the horseless reins, or the two dead persons, I didn't understand.

Then I knew.

There, faintly around the wreckage, a greenish hue mist spread across the accident. It came from Elizabeth's palms, concealing debris.

Her face, while still grief stricken, also showed horror. She swept the area with her eyes, frantically tossing around her head and kept glancing at her hands. When she realized that the green fog came from her, she rubbed her fingers together. Then she blew on them. Nothing she did stopped the green from expanding.

Elizabeth's eyes bugged and sweat beaded across her forehead. That's when she knew she was different. She probably always sensed it, but seeing green ribbons flow from her own palms clinched the notion.

Bells screeched in the distance, causing Elizabeth to glance in the direction they came. She drew in a deep breath and closed her eyes. As she relaxed, and by the time the police carriage arrived, all traces of the green vanished.

Eventually, someone led Elizabeth away. The gruesome accident was cleaned and the scene faded back to the present.

I was sure Elizabeth was scared about what had happened to her husband and, more importantly, what she had done.

"Now you understand why I went to go see Jane and

Sarah," Elizabeth said to me even though I was invisible. "I had to find answers." She stopped sweeping the kitchen floor.

I frowned feeling her sadness and made myself visible.

"I heard rumblings of some local women with special 'gifts,'" she continued, my sudden appearance not bothering her in the slightest. "So I asked around, discreetly of course. Eventually I got Jane's address. And you know the rest of the story."

"You can see me?"

"Of course." She nodded. "I've known since yesterday you were there and following me."

"How?"

"I saw your golden aura. You're like a miniature beacon of light. My own personal star."

I pondered this and wondered if there were others in the past who knew of my presence. And it made me pause that we both compared each other to stars.

"Was that the first time you used your gifts?" I asked.

"No. When I was a little girl, I suspected I was different. I could change the color of leaves with just a touch, escalate the temperature of water to boil instantly, and make flowers bloom fuller and brighter. A normal girl isn't supposed to do those things."

"And how did you come to know how to do any of it?"

"Trial and error," Elizabeth said as a chime filled the small room. "I did try to freeze water, but it never worked.

It would only turn slightly under room temperature." She stepped to the oven and removed a fresh-baked apple pie. "Of course I never told a soul or did any of these things out in the open. After the flower incident, I tried to raise a bird from the dead. It didn't work. Maybe it was because I wasn't strong enough, but I didn't want to practice and get found out. I'd be sent away to an asylum or something. So I stopped altogether . . . until *that* day. I almost forgot about my gifts."

"Do you know where your power comes from?" I pulled out a wooden chair and sat. "I've seen others like you in my travels around the world. None here, though. Not until I met you three, but now I've made a point to watch for others like yourselves. Most of them I came across in Europe. Maybe you're a descendent from one of them?"

"Maybe. My heritage is from England."

"Ah, so that explains it. The question I would have is where the original witches got their gifts."

"You'd have to ask Jane that. I honestly don't know. She told me about a brief history of the Salem Witches, so maybe she knows more. I'm pretty sure she does, she just doesn't share unless you need to know."

Nine

A few days passed and my life became a routine. I accepted Elizabeth's offer and stayed at her bungalow. My comings and goings didn't seem to bother her, even though she knew exactly when I was at her house and when I wasn't. That still messed with my wings.

While I traveled around the city, sometimes invisible, learning the layout, the smells, and its inhabitants, something pulled at me. I couldn't put my wings on it yet, but I would get to the bottom of my misgivings.

Evil would show its face.

Putting that gut feeling aside for now, I resumed my search for the girl.

As I walked along the main street, I ended up standing

in front of the city's government building. People milled about with stacks of parchment paper, quills, and ink jars. Murmurs flooded my ears about a small group of bad ordinaries.

My wings perked up, but I cautioned them to remain hidden along with my body.

A young child was led into the building escorted by two tall, muscular men. Her wrists bound in front of her frail body. Why would this girl need guards? She couldn't have been more than ten years old.

"Get inside, witch," the dark haired man said as he shoved the little girl through the wooden door.

"I am not a witch," she said, holding her head high in defiance.

"That's not what we hear," said the escort. "Now move!"

Could she be one of Elizabeth's friends' daughters?

The more I looked into the girl's soul, the telltale sign of her possessing magic flared right before my eyes. She had a small presence of fairy in her. Of course, that made me follow the party inside.

The men led the child into a large room. At the front sat a man in a black robe. Off to the side, twelve chairs had been placed, but were vacant.

Others from inside the building stood near the back to witness.

"Come forward, witch." The robed man waived his hand. "Stand before me."

Slowly, the child shuffled to the front of the room. The two men must have thought she didn't walk fast enough. At the last second, Dark Hair pushed her the final few feet. She fell to the ground, trying to catch herself with her bound hands.

"Get up you silly, little girl!" Dark Hair yelled. "Show some respect."

"I will when I see someone worth my respect." She glared up at the man.

"I see how you are," Robe Man said. "Your neighbors have turned you in for practicing witchcraft. They have witnessed many odd things about you. You have no friends, you don't go to school, you—"

"That does not make me a wi—"

"Silence!" His hand raised. "I will not have you question me or this court.

Ah, so I'm at this girl's *trial*.

"If I am being tried, where is the jury? Where are my peers? Where are my parents?"

"No one wanted to sit here, but trust me, they all have condemned you, including your parents." He stood and towed over her, shaking his fisted hand into her face. "So I must comply with their wishes." Returning to his seat, he drew in a breath. His eyes unfocused for a split second.

But I caught the slight movement. I searched the room, checking for demons.

None were found.

Then black smoke rolled up from behind the robed man. I shot forward ready to make the people flee from the building, but no char smell filled the air. I relaxed.

The ink-like ribbons bathed the judge in darkness, then seeped into his skin.

"No evidence?" the girl asked. "No witnesses? No trial?"

"You are sentenced to death, Abigail Williams," Robed Man said in a monotone voice, ignoring her questions.

They couldn't just kill an innocent child without any indication of wrong doings. This was the new England where people had freedom to practice religion, freedom from tyranny, and freedom from persecution. This wasn't right.

I flew back to Elizabeth's.

She only nodded as I was quickly retelling her everything I witnessed.

"That's why we have to be diligent at being secretive. I've heard that some witches were being tried without a formal hearing or jury."

"But that's the injustice of it. Everyone should be outraged!" I slammed my fist onto the table. "They sentenced a little girl to die based on nothing."

"I know. We should hurry and tell Jane and Sarah. I'm sure they know the girl and her family." Elizabeth grabbed her shawl. "I can't believe her own parents . . ."

We walked in silence to Elizabeth's friends' house. Thankfully it didn't take us long when we knocked. The door swung open on its own.

"Come in, both of you," Jane said. "I've heard already about Abigail."

"How?" I asked.

"Her mother is my sister."

My mouth dropped open.

"My sister knows what I am, but I didn't think she would turn in her own flesh and blood." Jane shook her head. "I can't believe it."

"Do you think your sister will turn you in?" Elizabeth asked?

"Now? I honestly don't know. So we must really be careful. Trust no one."

I came to know Elizabeth, Jane, and Sarah as friends and then watched them hung for their crimes for being witches. It wasn't right and didn't sit well with me. Not that I could have stopped it. I learned long ago to not intervene, but it didn't mean I couldn't be distraught about their deaths. I knew what they were: half-fairies. They didn't mean harm to anyone. The witches tried to keep to themselves. They only performed their magic in the confines of the forests, and, on rare occasion, in someone's home. Besides, most were half-Summer fairies and needed the earthly elements. They were harmless.

Like any species, there were a few bad witches. I found

out a few were from the Winter realm. They had created the unusual rainy summer that year.

The trials held in Salem executed nineteen, most of them women, fifty people confessed to being witches, over a hundred were imprisoned, and more than two hundred were accused of the witching craft.

I knew the truth of the trials, the accusations, and the unjust imprisonments.

Sammael was behind it. He must have thought one of the witches could be the girl to release him from his prison.

Or be his pawn.

I would have thought he'd want out of his cell.

He had whispered into the ears of the clergy, the area mayors, and the important persons of the town. It was he who condemned the women in hopes to stop the Redeemer.

There must be another reason why he was seeking the girl, too.

Part
2

Ten

June 24, 1997, 3:26 P.M.
St. Joseph, Minnesota

After my time on the East Coast and getting to know Elizabeth, I was ready for another change. I didn't want to be someone's imaginary friend or meet them just before they died. I wanted a real life experience. I wanted to have human interaction. I needed to walk in their shoes, as Michael had once told me to do.

The tiny wail of a newborn baby vibrated deep into the earth's core. My wings hummed with it, and I wondered if *the* babe had been born. I remembered Sidelle had said the earth would tell her somehow. This could be the earth's way and I only had to listen.

The vibration grew more intense and an unforeseen pull tugged me toward Minnesota. All I knew was that people called it the land of ten thousand lakes.

As I neared the state's border, my wings fluttered erratically and my body landed in St. Joseph. It was a small town just north of the Twin Cities. I flew to a ranch-style yellow house on a cul-de-sac. A tug made me enter the residence. I perused many pictures of a young married couple. A tall woman with her hand over an extended belly. She stood beside a shiny, green car and a man with a warm smile on his face.

There was something special about this couple. I could sense it. The love could be seen in their eyes for each other and the baby she carried. As I looked around the house, clothes were thrown across various pieces of furniture. Dresser drawers open. Beds not made. They were in a hurry to get some place.

I remained invisible and circled above the town in search for a hospital or a structure with the letter "H" on the roof. I hovered outside a window of a small, brick building. There lay in the bed, the woman from the picture. Her husband sat next to her, wiping her forehead. Lying in the mother's arm, a pink blanket showed the face of a tiny baby sucking on little fingers.

When I entered the maternity room, white light encompassed the newborn baby. I had never seen that before. From the expression of the parents' faces, they must not have seen anything strange about the girl in their arms. I slowly approached the bedside and peered into the baby's face. Her lids opened revealing brown eyes and they gazed into mine.

In my mind, I saw flashes of her as a toddler and then as a teenager. But then nothing of her into adulthood.

A heavy feeling washed over me. Why couldn't I see past her college years?

The mother moved, switching the baby to her other arm. As she did, a pudgy hand reached for me. I didn't think babies did that.

I touched her soft, rosy cheek and then she cooed. Her parents smiled. Something about the girl's eyes, the way she smiled. Like it was only for me, and that small reach; it all spoke directly to my soul. I wished to be here for her. Even if she wasn't the Redeemer, I wanted—no, needed—to watch her grow. It saddened me that she wouldn't be an adult, but maybe with me at her side, she'd overcome the odds.

A rustle from my hidden wings caused me to pay attention. Something else was here in the room with us. An evil presence I hadn't felt since that time in Europe when a Winter Fairy's friend crossed my path.

Sorrow, then anger swept through me.

No angel felt depression so I knew there was someone else causing this. Then the eerie feeling subsided.

Another rumble shook deep within the earth.

And I knew this was another signal. This girl was special.

I sent a message to Sidelle. *"Hell's gates are open and they have unleashed the Demons. Be ready."*

She never acknowledged my communication, but I knew I'd see her again.

Soon, too.

"She's not breathing," the mother screamed, snapping me to the present. "Why is she not breathing? Go get help!"

The father bolted out the door, yelling for nurses and doctors. A few seconds later, he returned with a doctor in tow.

He checked the baby's breathing, still swaddled in her mother's arms.

"Code blue," yelled a doctor as he hit buttons on the wall.

"What's happening?" the mom asked.

"I don't know," the father said. "Let the doctors work. They'll save Zoe."

"Is she d—"

"Don't think like that. She'll be fine."

Zoe.

That's what they'd named her. I knew I shouldn't interfere with her life. When the body gave out, time was up. It's one of the hardest things to let happen. But I couldn't just stand there and do nothing. I couldn't let

Zoe's life slip into the heavens.

I wouldn't.

My hands clenched at my sides.

Before I realized it, my wings sprung out from my back. I whispered to the father to step away so I could take his place at the bedside. My wings cradled around the mother and child. I raised my hand and caressed Zoe's small head. White light filled my palm and spread into her.

Gentle hands from a nurse removed Zoe from her mother's arms as the crash cart moved to the side of the bed. Zoe was laid in a clear crib. More white coats added to the frenzy as orders were shouted.

My Light continued to pour into Zoe's body as I stood over her.

She gulped in air, then wailed.

The nurses sighed. "She's fine now," a doctor told the parents. "Not sure what happened, but your little girl is breathing again. We will run some more tests to find out more information."

As the hospital staff left with Zoe, I watched the family settle back down. Relief on their faces.

Then a familiar power surged into the room. Michael's glorious gray wings appeared, expanding from wall to wall. I checked over my shoulder to look at the family. Their heads tilted toward each other. The father comforting his wife.

"I'm sorry," I said before Michael could rebuke me. "I

had to. There is something about Zoe . . . I couldn't let her die."

My mentor moved closer to me, but didn't say a word.

"There was an evil here in the room right before Zoe died. She needed to be saved." I nodded as I waited for Michael to speak.

"You call her by her name?" Michael asked.

"Yes—"

"In all the centuries you've been watching over children, this is the first time I've heard you use the girl's name when you speak of them." He smiled. "You feel connected to her. Why do you think that is?"

"I don't know. I just feel . . . I know there is something more about this one than I've ever felt in the past."

"Follow your heart then, Kieran. It will always lead to good."

"You aren't going to reprimand me for bringing her back to life?"

"No. You've never done it before and I can assume you will never do it again. While I don't think you'll see it as punishment, you are to stay with this girl and keep an eye over her. If there was an evil presence here, she'll need a guardian. And I can't think of a more perfect angel than you."

Eleven

A few days later, after the doctors cleared Zoe of any health problems, they discharged the mother from the hospital. I watched as Zoe's parents created a cozy baby room for her on a main-floor bedroom, facing the cul-de-sac. They had painted the walls pale lavender and moved in a white sleigh crib, changing table, and matching dresser.

Their life was filled with happiness. Zoe was the perfect baby for them. She hardly ever fussed or cried. Her face wore a smile all the time. It could have been because I was always at her side.

People would stop her parents and tell them "how fortunate they were to have such a happy and content baby" or "how lucky they were for having an easy first child." What those strangers didn't know was how close the parents had been to hosting a funeral instead of a baby shower.

Zoe's aura had also changed. When I first saw her, she had a white glow. Now as she grew older, it was changing to purple. I didn't know what that meant, but it couldn't be good.

I knew I'd be in her life for as long as she needed me to. So I came up with a game plan. Nudging the owners of a house a few yards away, I suggested they pack their belongings and move across town, leaving me the perfect opportunity to set up shop. Of course, I couldn't pull this off alone. I needed help.

Michael and his first lieutenant, Terah, came to my call.

"I need you guys to pose as my parents," I explained. "I'm going to befriend her, so I can be by her side all the time. Since she's still young now, you probably don't need to be really seen, but I'd like you both to meet her parents and stage a few run-ins. You could wave to Zoe's parents when they go on their nightly walk, or run into them at the grocery store. And I thought we could buy this place." I pointed to the white house we stood in front of. "It would be the control base for all of us as new information comes in."

"I see you've taken my advice about being a leader to a whole new level," Michael said. "Whatever you think you'll need; you only have to ask. We'll make it work."

"Agreed," Terah said. "I like your idea. We may have to add to the house if there's going to be a lot of traffic here. And it could be a safe place for our Nephilim soldiers."

"We should place a telecommunicator someplace on the property in case the Nephilim needs to contact the Archangels," I suggested.

"Great idea, Kieran," Michael said. "We'll have an angel sculpture commissioned in the garden."

"How will that exactly work?"

"She'll be the eyes and ears of the house."

"I don't understand."

"You will."

My plan worked brilliantly. Michael and Terah bought the house and I contacted a construction company. After many more nights of meetings, we agreed that another floor should be added, along with the state-of-the-art surveillance and security system. Terah also hired a gardener to landscape a spectacular backyard.

In the center of the large lawn, Michael created a fountain surrounding a white, marble angel, her majestic wings extended and arms reaching toward the sky. Her stone eyes gazed into the heavens with an incredibly real expression. She looked as if she were in the midst of a conversation, maybe speaking to God.

Then Terah stood next to Michael. They filled their hands with water, said a prayer, and let the water fall across the statue's feet.

The minute the prayer ended, the angel stirred. Her massive wings contracted, then expanded again. She moved her head down and looked at the Archangels, nodded and went back to her original pose.

Paschar became the backyard focal point and I was glad to have a little reminder of Heaven placed with me on Earth.

Three months later as final construction neared, Michael and Terah didn't have to go out of their way to meet any of the neighbors. They eventually made introductions to them. I, of course, kept myself invisible most of the time.

One day I had a chance to walk beside little Zoe. I peered under the stroller's cover. Her eyes were closed, but then snapped open and a huge smile spread across her chubby face when she saw me. I knew she could see me even though I remained invisible. We were connected and it had nothing to do with me saving her life. Well, okay, maybe it did a little bit.

She squirmed out from under her Disney printed blanket and reached for me.

"You'll guard her well, Kieran," Terah said. *"She gravitates toward you, too."*

"I will do so with my life."

The first few years watching over Zoe were easy. She never left the safety of her parents' side. At my request, the Archangels placed protective wards around their house. As Zoe aged, more angels descended upon the town. If angels could sense her, then maybe so could demons.

And Sammael.

I knew when she grew to school age, things would change. But I'd enjoyed my time with her nonetheless. I became her imaginary friend, to my chagrin. To her, I appeared as a skinny, eight-year-old boy with light blond hair and blue eyes. We'd sit in her room for hours and play with My Pretty Ponies, dress up Barbie dolls, and because her parents didn't just give her only girly toys, we even played with Transformer action figures.

During the summer weekends, Kevin and Jackie took Zoe up north to their cabin. Of course, I also went with; they just never knew. But Zoe sure did.

I was with her in the little, red paddle boat to make sure we didn't tip over. When she went swimming in the crystal clear lake so that she'd always resurface. Even while Zoe went scrounging in the muck for turtles to race during the local festivals.

I knew our playtime was coming to a close as she neared her fourth birthday.

"I'm going to school tomorrow," Zoe pouted as she showed me her new purple backpack. "I wish . . . I wish. Never mind, it's dumb."

"Nothing you say is ever silly."

"I don't wanna go to school. I wanna stay here with you and play with my toys."

"Zoe, you don't ever have to worry about being alone." I watched as big tears fell from her brown eyes.

It pained my heart.

"But people are going to think I'm weird talking to you when no one else can see you." She hiccupped. "Can you come to school with me?"

"If you want me to—"

"But you're older than me so we wouldn't be in the same class." She frowned. "Will others be able to see you? It doesn't matter. You'll still be my friend even if I don't make any, right?"

"Zoe." I pushed her chin up to look at me. "You'll be fine and lots of kids will become your friends."

"Promise?"

"Trust me."

Twelve

The next day Zoe's parents stood on their front porch and snapped pictures of their baby girl's first day of kindergarten. She wore a bright purple and white shirt with jean shorts. And strapped to her feet were brand new purple sneakers.

I watched as they loaded her into the car and drove away. I never had included Michael or Terah about this part of my plan. They'd probably think I was going overboard. As soon as the vehicle rounded the corner and turned onto Sandbar Lane, I couldn't stop myself. I had to go after her, staying invisible to watch over Zoe.

Of course I beat the Jabril family to the school's parking lot. I watched as other families dropped off their children.

Some kids cried, while others bounded away without a backward glance. I knew today was going to be tough for Zoe. Seeing a friendly, smiling face would help.

I scanned the playground. By the edge of the property, a girl with long, black hair stood, kicking a pebble with her toe. She kept glancing at the group of kids playing on the swings, but she didn't approach them. The small cluster of girls giggled and pointed at the lone girl. I was about to approach the girl when an itch on my back made me stop. The girl lifted her chin and looked right at me, but that was impossible. No one could see me. Right?

But then I heard the unique rumble from the Jabrils' vehicle pull into the parking lot.

I watched as Zoe jumped out of the minivan, scanned the playground, then turned and hugged her parents. With her head held high, she grabbed her My Pretty Pony lunchbox and school bag and walked straight into the cluster of girls.

"Hi, I'm Zoe." She stuck her little arm out to the nearest girl. "Are you in kindergarten, too?"

"I am. I'm Cali."

"And I'm Rena. Who do you have for a teacher, Zoe?"

"I have Ms. Daizy."

"We do, too!"

All the girls screamed and hopped up and down. Then the black-haired girl from the corner of the playground walked over to the group. My wings threatened to appear again, but I couldn't let that happen. I hadn't felt the need for them in years. Why now?

"I heard you have Ms. Daizy," she said. "I think I have her. I just moved here."

"Hi. I'm Zoe. And this is Cali and Rena. You can hang out with us if you want."

"Thanks. My name's Morgan."

A dark shadow swept over me that I didn't understand. But something in me told me to protect Zoe.

Morgan stepped closer to her.

A chill ran through me. And that was enough. I decided then to make a new plan. In my mind, I pictured myself as a five-year-old boy, looked around for the best hiding spot, and confirmed no one was looking my way.

I materialized behind a tree in time to witness Morgan grabbing Zoe's lunchbox, and about to open it, when I ran over to them and knocked Morgan down. I hadn't meant to push her that hard. The glare she gave me as she stood turned my blood cold. Then she smiled at me as she brushed off the tiny rocks against her legs.

"Sorry," I said. "I didn't mean to knock you over."

"Don't worry about it," Morgan said. "It's just a scrape, I'll be okay."

"Are you sure you're all right?" Extending my hand, I attempted to help her.

"Yeah." She didn't take my hand. "I just wanted to see her lunchbox."

Brushing off the icy feeling she still gave me, I faced Zoe.

Wide eyed, she stared at me. Mouth hanging open, she snapped it closed. The other girls stopped giggling and watched me.

"Are you new, too?" Cali asked. When I didn't answer she asked again, louder.

"Kieran?" Zoe whispered.

"You know him?" Rena asked.

"Yes! He's my Guard—"

"Neighbor," I interrupted.

"Do you have Ms. Daizy for a teacher?" Zoe showed me her room assignment.

"Yep." A grin spread across my face. "I do."

Just then the bell rang. Teachers corralled the students and shepherded them into the school, looking at the room assignment sheets as kids passed. Morgan, Rena, and Cali ran ahead. Zoe and I lingered a bit longer outside.

"Are you really here?" Zoe asked. "And not in my imagination?"

"Yes, I'm really here. I told you that you wouldn't be going to school alone."

"But—

"I'll always protect you." I wrapped my arm around her shoulder. "How did you know it was me?"

"Your eyes. They are bright blue like the sky. And I knew from your blond hair." She turned and hugged me.

"Oh, I just knew it was you!"

"Come on." I chuckled. "We'll be late on our first day of school."

"Okay, Bestie!"

We walked hand in hand through the double glass doors.

For a sneak peek into Sidelle's novella: *Fires & Fairies*, continue reading.

Chapter One

A staccato trumpet blast announced the exact moment when the change of seasons occurred. The double oak doors swung open with great ceremony, and King Oberon waltzed into the throne room, a glowing, pale blue scepter in his hand. His green robes flowed behind him, reminding me of a rolling prairie, billowing out behind him. His crown was entwined with white branches, and giant, dark green wings hung loosely around his body. He was the perfect picture of royalty.

Oberon silenced the horns with a wave of his massive hand. "Winter has ended," the Summer Fairyland king declared. "Let us join in celebration for the start of summer. May this exchange bring a bounty of wealth, growth, and prosperity."

The scepter now burned green, and he raised it high above his head before turning and placing the long metal staff on the altar near his throne.

On cue, flutes, fiddles, and drums raised an upbeat tempo, and the court exploded into song. Couples danced with their arms flowing around each other, and lone bodies swayed to their own beat. Some of the guests fluttered their wings, others cocooned themselves. House brownies streamed into the massive hall bearing plates of candied fruits, breads, and meats which they set on the royal table, which was already decorated with tall vases overflowing with fresh wildflowers. The delicious aroma of cheeses and buttery pastries wafted the air on the far side of the room.

I, on the other hand, stood alone with my back pressed against the wall and my fists clenched. The party would go on well into the night, but I had no intention of staying. I turned and blew out the candle sconce, needing to drape myself in darkness, then I wrapped my long, light green wings around my body. When I wasn't at a festival or party, I kept my wings hidden—unlike the fairies who chose to display them. The truth was that Fairies didn't need wings to fly, since we used glamour for that. Our wings only really need to come out when we experienced intense emotions.

I was almost out the door when my name was called. "Sidelle?" King Oberon's hand reached for me, caught my arm. "Where do you think you're slinking off to? Come and dance."

My nostrils flared. "Yes, Your Highness." I walked the few steps to the dais and placed a kiss on my father's cheek. Out of the corner of my eye, I saw the center of the scepter pulse to a soft green. "Just one. And then I'm outta here."

The king sighed with resignation. "I don't understand why you can't be a normal daughter. One who likes music and dances."

I shrugged, and he placed his hand on the small of my back, leading me to the center of the room. Multi-colored gowns and feathered masks parted before us like the sea.

"I do," I whispered, then inclined my head toward the onlookers. "Just not with all this."

"I wish you'd make friends with the nymphs and pixies I send you from court."

A lone flute played the first notes to a popular song, and some of the crowd lost interest in us. Instead, they turned back to watch the musicians or join in the dance.

"I can make my own friends," I told him for the millionth time. "I'm not going to fabricate friendships just to appease you." I bowed gracefully, preparing for the dance. "Besides, I have Brea."

He nodded reluctantly. "Yes, you have Brea. But you are a Lady of Summer. You need to have more than *one* friend." He opened his arms and I stepped into them. We swayed to the slow tempo, letting our wings extend to their full height.

"Maybe I don't want any," I told him.

His eyes rolled toward the ceiling. "What am I going to do with you?"

"Nothing."

"I must do *something*." The Summer king guided me into a quick spin, and my olive gown swirled around my legs, followed by my wings. He grabbed my hand and waist when I teetered, close to losing my balance. "Do you have a special someone?"

I glared, righting myself. "This again? Father, I am *not* having this conversation with you."

"There are plenty of nobles who would love to have your hand in marriage—"

Enough was enough. "I'm not ready," I snapped, stepping out of his grasp. I grabbed my green-feathered mask, meaning to fling it to the ground, but it caught in the waves of my black hair instead, cutting short my dramatic intent. "And don't you *dare* try arranging anything. I want to live life on my own terms."

"It's customary for all members of the Royal Court to have a lifelong partner. You should settle down—"

"I have eons before I must marry." I stuck one hand on my hip. "I don't understand why you keep insisting. We're immortal. There isn't any rush."

"As you wish." Oberon turned from me, but he always had to have the last word. "For now," he tossed over his shoulder as he stalked back to his throne, leaving me in a sea of brightly colored fairies.

I adjusted the mask to cover my face then stormed out of the masquerade, stewing over his last statement about marriage. I firmly believed someone would enter my life when the time was right, but until then, I would live on my own terms. I didn't need a fairy at my side, despite what my father said. In spite of my objections, every few hundred sundowns he raised the topic again, then set off on some fairy hunt to marry me off. So far I'd managed to squash all requests.

As far as my only having one friend, I saw absolutely nothing wrong with that. It had to be better than faking friendships with fairies that were only there because my father had instructed them to be there—or because they thought it would help their court status.

The lush gardens around Aestas Castle had begun to sprout, and their vivid colors glowed in the moonlight. Small flowers poked through the ground, and tree branches thickened with fresh buds. The soft new grass shoots invited me to touch them, so I removed my lace slippers, enjoying the squishy terrain beneath my bare feet. Encouraged by the warm breeze, I peeled off my shawl and let it fly into the wind.

As I walked the pathway toward the Wild Forest, sprites flew past, intent on cleaning the many statues. Some waved, others bowed toward me, and though I was in a hurry, I smiled back. In the distance, the moonlight shimmered like white magic on Lacus Pond. Every once in a while, something splashed on the surface, meaning the merfolk and water nymphs were probably frolicking. Goblins and gnomes romped the wooded grounds, scrounging for food and causing mischief, but I paid no attention to them.

The only thing on my mind was getting to my secret spot in the woods. I craved the peaceful atmosphere, away from prying eyes and fake smiles. In the woods I could be myself. I could say whatever thoughts crossed my mind. No one ever answered me, but that was okay.

When I finally arrived at my destination, I nestled onto the chair I'd fashioned a few seasons ago. The oak had stood solidly against the harsh winds and rain that sometimes pelted the area.

Yes, I was a fairy. But my life was not all about unicorns, rainbows, and parties, though—out of duty—I attended every royal event, no matter the size. There was hardly a night when something wasn't going on inside the castle or in the city of Aestas, whether we were throwing a royal festival or cheering up a pixie who had accidentally broken a flute. I was well aware that my father hated the sullen behavior I displayed whenever we received guests or listened to the problems of his subjects, but I never deviated. I had always been true to myself, and I knew deep down that the true me didn't quite fit in at Aestas Castle or at the royal outings. I much preferred to be in the forest. Alone.

In the peace and quiet of my favorite place, I remembered back to the celebration my father had thrown when I'd entered my fifth season. The whole city had been invited, of course, and all members of court had attended. I had been showered with gifts. Only one present still stood out in my memory, though. That was the gift which had shown me what I really was.

My one and only real friend, Brea, had given me parchment paper and some colored quills, and I'd used them to draw. Father discovered what I was doing, and though he wasn't angry, he seemed shocked that I could create pictures without glamour. But what choice did I have? When I was born, he'd sealed my magic. Since I was a Lady of the castle, it was important that I act properly. I couldn't be seen as a failure or someone who mistreated power. As a child I couldn't understand my powers or how to use them, so he'd kept them from me until I got older.

Brea's father hadn't sealed her glamour, so she taught me a few things over the seasons. One afternoon after that fifth birth's celebration, we sat in the garden, and I drew make believe worlds in which square towers loomed over the horizon and carriages moved without the aid of horses. On one side I swirled a lake of deep blue water, and on the other I created a vast green countryside. Brea guessed it was supposed to be a park, and she asked where it was since she'd never seen anything like it in Fairyland. When she told me my lake looked more like a fire pit, she was smiling. That's when she showed me a trick.

She held my hand palm side up, then cupped hers over mine. With her eyes twinkling, she said, "fire" then moved her hand away. Just like that, a green flame appeared, dancing in the center of my palm. Then she turned my wrist and said, "parchment" while tapping the area of water I had sketched on the paper. I stared in fascination as the flame transferred from my hand and hovered above the drawn lake like a sun.

Just then, the wind howled. It blew the green flame across the parchment and onto the grass. Real fire erupted and spread through the grass, hopping swiftly from branches to trees. Panicked, we flew to the castle for help and screamed the news to the first fairy we saw. Horns sounded, and a flurry of pixies and house brownies rushed to the garden. We ran back to watch, and my father materialized ahead of us. He snapped his fingers, and just like that the fire extinguished. Everything was as it had been before, with lush green grass and full flowering trees, though a charred stink lingered in the air.

It was then that my glamour training started. It was done under my father's guidance, and practiced in private. I guess he realized that my ignorance might be less dangerous than keeping me in the dark.

Chapter Two

The memory faded from my mind as I leaned down to replace my slippers. Just as I slipped my chilled toes in, a branch snapped behind me. My wings unfurled, startled by the sound, but I assumed it was just a sprite, climbing in a tree someplace nearby. When I heard nothing else, I contracted my wings and conjured my glamour, smiling to myself. I had come a long way since my first lesson.

As the glamour rose within me, my body tingled from head to toe, and my fingers pulsed, waiting to release my wishes. I focused, instructing the earth to open into a shallow pit then arrange wood fragments into a triangular stack. When all was prepared, I swept my hand over it and sent the green light. With the passing of seasons, and many days spent practicing, I had mastered fire. The green flames quivered in the slight breeze, not touching the twigs but casting a dancing light.

I stared into the glow, contemplating my current situation. If my father took matters into his own hands and forced me into a marriage, could I—

Another twig snapped much closer, and my skin prickled with alarm. My wings emerged from my back again, flapped twice, then slowed, fluttering slightly.

"Who's there?" I demanded, scanning the dense forest. "Come out. Slowly. I'm armed and I will—"

Leaves rustled nearby and more branches snapped.

Something approached from the direction of the pond. I stood my ground and materialized a bow and an arrow, squinting into the darkness to focus my vision. I saw a hand wrap around a branch just a few feet away and took aim, waiting. The shadow unfolded like a curtain, revealing a head, then a torso, and finally a pair of long, lean legs. They belonged to a young, male fairy in a blue tunic.

"Hello," he said quietly, speaking in a low, deep voice. Even in the dark I saw his eyes on me. "I'm sorry. I didn't mean to scare you."

I rolled my shoulders back, standing tall, and pointed the silver tipped arrow at his chest. "You didn't." My wings twitched, always on guard. "I don't scare easily."

"You shouldn't be out here alone." He stepped forward but kept his wings hidden from view. The strangest sensation came over me when he spoke. Somehow his voice resonated in my bones and wrapped around me like a blanket.

"Says you," I said, matter of fact, "who is also alone in the forest."

"Yes," he said, sounding amused. He took a few more steps toward me, but I didn't move. "So I am."

I adjusted my grip on the bow. "Don't—"

"I'm not here to hurt you, My Lady." Very slowly he reached out and lowered the tip of the arrow, watching my reaction as he did so. I was too surprised to object. "I saw the flames and came to investigate."

My Lady? Why would he have called me that? How did he know me? I didn't recognize him, and I thought I knew all the Summer fairies.

"Who are you?" I demanded, lowering the bow but keeping it notched. He didn't seem to mean me any harm, but I stayed alert.

"No one. I'm just passing through."

When he turned toward me, the light from the fire revealed his exquisite features. Straight black hair framed a square, handsome face, accenting the piercing blue of his eyes. The chest he partially hid beneath his tunic was beautifully sculpted, and he was tall, towering over me; my head came to just under his chin.

"You don't have a name?"

"What are you doing out here all alone?" he asked, scanning the area and avoiding my question. "You're far from the city's borders."

"I know where I am."

"You must live in the city if you know this area well." He raised an eyebrow and slid his hands into the front pockets of his tan breeches. "Come here often?"

I wasn't about to let him grill me with twenty questions. "I think you need to move on. Especially since you're 'just passing through.'"

"Of course." His smile was brief and apologetic. "I will leave you to . . . whatever it was you were doing." Without another word he brushed past me and headed deeper into the forest.

I stared after him, bewildered by the faint, cold feeling that lingered in his wake. It was odd that I had never seen him before, though I didn't know everyone in the city. He definitely didn't live in the castle, because I would have seen him there. On the other hand, maybe he was a recluse—like me—and didn't attend the festivities. For his sake, I hoped Father never found out that one of his subjects hadn't appeared at court when a royal decree had gone out.

I was intrigued. In all my seasons coming to this spot, I had never seen another fairy venture this far from the castle and into the forest. It wasn't safe for them. It wasn't safe for me either, but my glamour was more potent than theirs because of my stature, which was third in line to the Queen Mother of Aestas.

That was another reason why my magic had been sealed in my earlier seasons. When I was about ten seasons old, father had explained to me what my rank meant. In the line of successions, if something happened to my mother, the queen, I would assume her title. For as long as I could remember, my grandmother, the Queen Mother, had ruled. In fact, she'd held the position for as long as father had known her. When I asked father more questions, he waved them off, telling me not to worry about the complicated succession rules. Evidently the status hadn't changed since the start of the seasons, and maybe not even before that.

Fairies have existed since before time was measured. Even before I came to understand the concept of eternity, the only measurement of time we counted was the number of changes of seasons. I remembered telling Father on my sixteenth season that nothing could last forever, but he had corrected me. He said 'fairies are forever.' At the time, I'd pondered the idea and eventually replied, 'for all of eternity.'

And that was how we came to call ourselves Eternals.

Chapter Three

I looked around my secret hideaway, strangely uncomfortable. The male fairy had somehow poisoned the place, making me want to scout a new location. I smothered the flame and swept my hand to return everything to the way it had been. New blades of grass now stood where others had lain flat, and the wooden chair came apart as sticks and branches moved back to their original places.

I glanced toward the pond, decided against going that way, then headed in a different direction, walking farther away from my home but staying in Summer. Rustling movements of elfin cats, water kelpies, and various insects surrounded me as I walked deeper into the forest. I called a flame to my palm, letting the green light illuminate the path for me. A blue shimmer in the air caught my eye, slowing my pace, and I stepped gingerly through the underbrush. Trying not to make any noise, I pulled aside the branches of a dense shrub and peeked through.

The small clearing before me opened into a vast, divisive canyon, and the other side of the ravine was covered entirely by a cloudy haze. I had heard of the Mist, but I'd never seen it before and had no idea it was that close to the city. The Mist surrounded Summer and Winter, moving almost like a living, breathing creature, but it never interfered with the Scepter exchanges. Any other time, the Mist could harm fairies if you weren't careful. You could get lost and never be seen again.

Nevertheless, the swirling clouds felt eerie, and my mind screamed at me to leave this place and never return. My wings twitched, eager to take me away, but some kind of force held me in place.

I tried to recall what had brought me here initially. Ah, yes. The glint of something blue.

I checked the area around me for any threat before I moved out onto the plateau, but apparently I didn't look hard enough. As soon as I stepped a little farther in I spied the stranger I'd met earlier. He sat on the edge, his long legs dangling over the side. The leather wrapped hilt of his sword peeked out from a black scabbard that crossed his muscular back.

I advanced on him as quietly as I could, not wanting to disturb him. I wasn't sure why I thought I shouldn't intrude, though. After all, he had stolen *my* safe place.

"I know you're there," he said, staring into the Mist. "I heard you as soon as you broke through the line of bushes."

"Oh, um . . ." My cheeks reddened and I searched for something intelligent to say. Unfortunately, all I came up with was, "Is . . . is this where you were headed?"

"No." He finally glanced up. When he saw I was watching him, his hands cupped something, then quickly slid whatever it was into his pocket.

"Can you not cross the canyon?" I asked. I walked to the edge and kicked a pebble, sending it into the pit, but I never heard it hit bottom.

"I don't know," he admitted. "I've never been so far into—"

My green eyes met his blue ones, asking.

"I'm a long way from home."

"Maybe there's a bridge," I suggested. I craned my neck, looking either for a way over the canyon, but saw nothing. "You could use glamour to make one, or you could just fly across." Turning back toward him, I almost slipped. I threw out my arms for balance then kicked off my slippers. "I hate these stupid things."

He chuckled at my clumsiness. "Glamour doesn't work in the Mist. It may be sketchy even being this close. Didn't you know that?" His long legs kicked the side of the plateau. "Doesn't matter. I'll make my way around it."

I didn't miss the fact that he'd laughed at me, but he was full of interesting information. And no, I hadn't known glamour didn't work there. I suppose I should have, but there was no reason for me to know. No one ever ventured into the Mist on purpose.

"*Around* the Mist?" I asked, confused. "It stretches for many sun ups and downs." I frowned. "Actually, does it even end?"

He shrugged, still staring off into the gray fog. "I have

all eternity to find out."

"When you put it that way." I let my breath out slowly. "Why did you leave home?" I blurted out, then I slapped my hand over my mouth.

"I'm sorry. You don't have to answer. I was just curious. I didn't mean to pry."

His handsome face twisted with something like disgust. "I'm just so sick of all this, you know?" He shook his head then scanned me from head to toe. One corner of his mouth curled briefly, but he didn't look like he was really laughing. "No, you definitely don't know what I mean. From the look of you, you live for parties, dressing up, and—"

"You don't know me!" I huffed, sweeping my hands down the front of my gown. "You think that just because I look like this I couldn't possibly understand? You have no idea." I scowled right back at him and pinched the stiff material clamped to my waist. "I wear this because my father tells me to. Otherwise, I wouldn't be wearing anything so extravagant. I mean, have *you* ever had to wear one of these?"

"Uh . . . no."

"Then you can't say anything." I glared at him until he looked away. Having won that round, I felt a little silly. Why I had gotten so upset with a complete stranger? Why did it matter what he thought? I changed direction. "Are you going to tell me your name now?"

"Are you?"

How irritating. Couldn't he answer a single question without asking another one? "I asked first."

"Fine," he finally said, softening at last. "It's Finnegan." He tilted his head and squinted my way, then patted the ground, motioning for me to sit.

I hesitated, then hiked up my skirt and plopped down next to him. It made no sense to argue with him, after all. "I'm Sidelle," I said, smoothing out my skirt. "What are you doing out here?"

"Exploring."

I lifted one brow and regarded him as if he were crazy. "In the Wild Forest then into the Mist? Are you on a death mission?"

He shrugged, not smiling. "It's how I get my kicks."

I became aware that I hadn't heard the sound of a single bird or animal since I'd arrived here. It made me wonder what kinds of predators lived in the Mist. Out here, beyond the shelter of the forest, the sky was black, but the grayish haze provided a vague light. I conjured a green fire, but it sputtered out. Using more glamour, I threw a fire ball and sent it floating over the canyon, close to the Mist side. It flickered, and I pulled it toward the center of the ravine where it barely lit the area with a green hue.

"Won't your father wonder where you are?" Finnegan asked.

"Probably." I nodded. "He won't send the search party—"

His body tensed beside me. "Search party?" He shook his head violently. "No! No one can find me." He jumped to his feet then dragged me up and pushed me toward the forest. "You need to leave now!"

"Whoa." I righted myself before I could fall over. "Hold on. You can't tell me what to do. You don't own this spot." I pointed to the ground. "Last time I checked, this was my—"

"Fine. Then *I'll* leave." He stalked away, following the edge of the canyon, then stopped and yelled back, "And don't follow!"

"Follow you?" I shouted at his retreating back. "Who do you think you are? I wouldn't follow you if you were the last Summer fairy in Aestas!"

"Good!" came his reply.

He was the most obnoxious fairy I'd ever met. No wonder he was running away from something. With a personality like that, I bet he didn't have any friends.

I extinguished the firelight, blinked, and ended up in my bedroom.

Continue reading for a sneak peek at the first few chapters of Finn, the Winter Prince's story: *Poisons & Princes*!

Chapter One

A massive green dragon emerged from the southernmost turret of Aesculus Castle, the center of Winter, a magnificent golden carriage cradled between its iridescent wings. Before it waited a procession of Summer fairies, and their double rows moved forward at a snail's pace as the iced gate swung open. The beast carried the season's offerings from Summer: an array of wild flowers, baskets of dried fruits, and a pale yellow, glowing scepter. The dragon tossed its head, snorting its frustration, but pomp and circumstance couldn't be rushed. The longer Summer held the scepter, the longer the warm weather and sunny days lasted.

In turn, when Winter fairies traveled to Summer, we took our time. Neither group used Glamour—Fairy magic—to travel through the lands for the exchange.

Aesculus Castle, my home, was nestled between a snow-covered mountain and a bottomless cliff. The only road was a narrow pathway suspended high above the canyon, separating the frozen tundra from the city limits. The castle walls were made of solid, glistening ice, and its enormous gate was carved from a three-foot thick block of ice. A frosty mist blanketed the entire land, making it impossible for the members of the procession to see more than a few feet past their own hands, but I could see them just fine. A few Summer fairies slipped on the ice, but the dragon's large claws gripped the road, protecting all who rode inside the carriage.

The parade left a trail of steam in their wake. Personally, I could never understand how Fairies could live in a warm place like Summer. The few times I'd been there, my body hadn't been able to adjust to the smoldering temperature. I'd had to return to the Winter's borders every thirty sundowns or so, where I recharged for at least four or five sundowns. My last trip there had taken a heavy toll on me. To be honest, it knocked me right on my ass.

I was not my mother's favorite Fairy at the moment. Tired of my regimented life within the castle walls, I—the Prince of the Winter Court—had run from home, leaving my court responsibilities behind. It was somewhat of an understatement to say Queen Mab was not happy. Not at all. But I had succeeded, and eventually I had found my way into the Summer lands. That's where I'd met Sidelle, the daughter of King Oberon. She'd handed me over to her father—which I had to admit was the responsible thing to do—and he'd kept me captive in Aestas' dungeons. In the end, I had been moved to the 'guest' wing of the Summer castle, but I remained their prisoner until one of the Winter knights came to collect me and bring me back to Mab.

Summer fairies and Winter fairies were not friends. In

fact, we only met twice a year, at the change of seasons. It was a brief but elaborate ceremony, and every detail must be followed or else things could go very wrong. The rules for the scepter exchange were few but rigid, and when the lines were recited incorrectly by the Winter representative one year, and the scepter did not turn the appropriate color of green, Queen Mab and the Winter fairy knights had gone on a hunt for the culprit. That's when I'd made my escape.

While I was being held as a prisoner in Summer, I learned about unfrozen water and picnics, and I even took an actual boat ride. Back in Winter, we had other experiences, like riding snow off cliffs or playing intense games of snowball fights and having icicle sword duals that often turned into blood baths. In Summer, I experienced warm sunlight on my face and a hot breeze caressing my body. Everything about it made my skin crawl. The heat turned my body ashen, it stole my breath, and when I thought it couldn't get any worse, I landed on a smoldering island that drained me of so much Glamour that death called to me. Delle—that's the nickname I'd given the beautiful Sidelle—had saved me by infusing some of her Summer essence into me.

After that, we proclaimed our love to each other.

Then I bailed.

Actually, I didn't really bail, but I couldn't return to her as I'd promised. Which was why I was now living back in

Winter full time.

An ice shattering shriek from the dragon jerked my thoughts back to the trees lining the corridor inside the gates. Their branches were so thickly draped by icicles they looked like shiny weeping willows. A hint of rain lingered in the air, but I couldn't figure out if it came from the Summer fairies or from us. After all, ice was only frozen water. Loud, harsh music floated around the castle, the notes banged on iced drums, indicating Winter's festivities had started. Curious Winter fairies began to appear in the halls. Some courageous members of my world tossed ice shards or dared trip a convoy member, but for the most part they left Summer alone.

The curtain on the carriage swept open, and a slender hand reached out. A beautiful face peered out, framed by long, ebony black hair which had been swept into an up-do, and lit by brilliant green eyes.

I stared, dumbstruck. Sidelle was here as the Summer representative. Was this some kind of sick joke? Why would Oberon send her, of all fairies?

Normally I would dawdle and arrive late to the Exchange, but this changed everything. Delle was here in my castle. I had to see her, to explain—but I had to be careful with Mab so close. Using Glamour, I quickly dressed in my royal attire—black breeches and a dark blue tunic—and strapped my faithful sword across my back. I rushed through the castle to greet our guests, coming up with an idea as I ran toward the Great Hall. On impulse, I grabbed the first female fairy to cross my path and drew her close.

"Do as you're instructed," I whispered to her.

"And what will you give me in return, my Prince?" she asked coyly.

"A favor."

She smiled. "Ooh. Something must be going on with you to grant me that." She turned away, letting her navy skirt twirl around her legs. "I wonder what it could be?"

I chuckled. "Nothing."

I ushered her into a corner where the procession would pass, planning to get a good glimpse of Sidelle. But our two bodies couldn't quite fit in the small alcove. The fairy I was with peered back at the incoming procession of Summer fairies, and her eyes widened.

"It's … her, isn't it? She's come into Winter." She beamed at me. "Maybe to see you?"

I hadn't planned on this kind of complication. "You're wrong," I snapped.

"Am I?" She giggled so loud the sound echoed off the walls like bells. "I don't think so! Why do you suppose Mab has been so … let's say, 'festive' these sundowns?"

"Keep your voice down!"

She batted my hand away from her face.

"Welcome to Aesculus Castle!" Queen Mab's shrill voice bounced and echoed off the walls.

I froze, but not before I managed to slap my hand over my companion's mouth.

"You are late," my mother continued, "and this will not go unnoticed. When you return to Summer, tell your king that I'll hold the scepter longer next time. See if that will teach you to waste my night."

She stepped out from behind an iced wall, her black hair flowing like a cape past her waist. She wore a blue embellished gown the color of a glacier, and her flashing eyes matched it perfectly. "The exchange must happen when the land dictates it," she said. "And She has spoken. Now you must hurry to the altar."

Obviously she didn't know my Delle.

"We will arrive when we are good and ready," Sidelle informed her. "If your subjects hadn't badgered us at the gate, we would have been in the courtyard sooner."

Mab's dark eyes reflected off the walls like a prism, and I shrank deeper into the corner.

"How *dare* you speak to me with such disrespect?" The queen's large, dark blue wings appeared, and she hovered near the howdah. "Who do you think you are, little fairy?" She drew herself up to be as large as she could, trying to intimidate Sidelle and remind her of the dire situation. "I am Queen Mab of the Winter court, and I demand respect! You are just the Summer rep."

Sidelle lifted her head high and drew in a breath before speaking. "I am not of your court. I do not bow to you or to your demands. As a Lady of Summer, you would be wise to speak to me as my title demands. Now, please lead me to the altar so we may do the exchange."

"You will speak to me with respect," Mab hissed, "as my title is higher than yours." Her eyes narrowed, and she leaned closer to Sidelle. "I will remember this, *Lady,* and I have a very long memory. It would be wise of you to consider that." Still looking furious, she turned away and led them toward the altar.

The backdrop was spectacular: snowcapped mountains beneath swirling crystals which seemed to dance on air, and a frozen lake stretching to the horizon. A frozen gazebo stood in the center, surrounded by a slab of solid ice at least ten inches thick. This was the altar for the Exchange.

I crept out from the corner, shooed the unknown female Fairy away, and followed the procession, staying behind it. Radiating disapproval, the Queen led the Summer fairies down a long hallway, then motioned for them to stop at the Grand Ballroom. After that, Mab directed Sidelle through the outer courtyard and toward the back yard of the castle.

"I see my representative is also late," the Queen said, looking annoyed. "He seems to do that a lot lately."

That was my cue. I appeared by the altar and nodded to my mother.

"I will go then," she said, sounding smug. "I think you

two may have some catching up to do, yes?"

Sidelle glanced at me and emotion swept over her beautiful face. Then she lowered her eyes and walked reluctantly toward the altar—and me.

I spoke first, since I was the one who had broken my promise. My head remained bowed, but I watched her. "I'm sorry, Delle. I couldn't meet you after … Well, you know."

Our eyes locked, and I saw raw emotions tearing through hers. I knew exactly where they came from. I, too, remembered the countless late nights we'd shared. I still felt the tingle on my lips from our first kiss, and I remembered the moment when we'd spoken those three precious words. I'd confessed my love to her, then I'd fled and hurt her further by not returning to Summer.

But I'd had a reason to go home. After being drained of nearly all my essence, I'd needed a massive recharge— even more than I could take from another Winter fairy. That moment had been the closest I'd ever come to death, even though fairies couldn't die. Still, we could become walking shells of nothing if enough of our Glamour and essence was taken.

"I did try a couple of times," I said, "but Mab blocked me."

Her eyes glittered with tears. She took a step away from me then stopped. Green wings sprung out behind her, and tears trickled down her pink cheeks. "I really don't want to hear it." She wiped her face with the back of her hand. "We have a job to do, so let's just forget about the past and focus."

"Delle. I owe you—"

She shook her head. "Don't." Her voice cracked, and I felt her pain deep in my chest. "Don't call me that."

"Mab found out where I had spent all my time and prevented me from returning to Summer," I pleaded. I needed her to understand, to forgive me. "When she figured out I was sneaking out to be with you, she blew her crown right off her head." I reached for her, but she stepped away. Until that moment, I had no idea anything could be so painful. "Please believe me, Delle. I really wanted to see you again, but she threatened to freeze me solid. I couldn't—"

"What do you want me to say?" She shrugged. "I don't care."

But she did care. The reality of that was plain on her beautiful face, on the tension around her sparkling eyes, on the tight, restrained line of her mouth, on the way she kept swallowing with effort. All I wanted was to comfort her, to assure her I hadn't meant to hurt her, that I still meant those three words.

Above us the sun glistened then pulsed, telling us we didn't have long before the ceremony at the altar must be completed. "Finn, just say your part so I can go home."

I blinked and cleared my throat. "This isn't over, Delle."

Sidelle said nothing as she presented me with the silver scepter. Together we placed it on the ice altar and waited. The center orb glowed white, pulsing occasionally with a soft yellow.

"Each snowflake is like the heart of Earth's memories," I recited, watching her all the time. "They fall to cover her body in a white blanket. Quietness fills the frosty air. The stillness of Winter's shadow makes way for a new season. Change brought to bring new life."

Sidelle stared at the scepter, unwilling to look at me, then took a deep breath. "Snow and ice will coat the pine tree's bough," she said in her turn, removing her hand from the scepter. "The birds won't sing their melodic song. Summer remains but must leave. Summer must resign. Winter, I ask you wake from under your wintry cover. You have waited long enough."

When the scepter pulsed to a radiant blue, we both knew the script had been said correctly, unlike at the exchange when I'd met her so long before. She didn't look at me before she turned away. I watched her retreating back and vowed never to hurt her again. And I would never allow her to walk away from me again, either. Not like that.

Chapter Two

The beginning of Winter festivities lasted long into the next sundown and the sundown after that, but I couldn't celebrate properly. It was in my blood to wish it could always be cold and snowing, and for me this was no joyous occasion.

For me, there was only her. I couldn't get her out of my head. I saw her eyes, her shock of black hair, those beautiful green wings ... and the look she gave me when she walked away and didn't turn back.

Sidelle.

She was all that mattered. Somehow I had to win her back.

Sure, I'd messed up royally, but I couldn't believe it would ruin my chances forever. Fairies are Eternals, so I couldn't hope to believe I'd been the love of her existence, but it had been the start of something great. I had felt it. So why hadn't I tried harder to get back to her? Well, Mab had threatened me. She hadn't come out and forbidden me to see her again, but she had definitely said I couldn't go back to Aestas.

Sidelle and I still had to overcome the fact that Summer and Winter didn't mix. That didn't truly matter—at least, that was what I told myself. In reality, it did. I didn't know of any Winter Fairy who had ever fallen in love with our sworn enemy. But ... was I still entirely

Winter? When Delle had forced her essence into me on that island, something had happened. I was different now. A part of me had changed. Maybe it was all in my mind, but I didn't think so. Not even now. When I had returned to Winter and stepped across the imaginary line into Aeculus' boarders, my body hummed with what I'd thought was excitement. But things changed for me. The longer I remained in Winter, the more I felt … off. A small part of me yearned to inhale the smell of a rainy day, feel the sun's rays on my face.

I refused to give in to Summer's temptations, however. I buried myself deeper inside the Castle, hoping to hang onto the old me.

Had I really blown it? At the Exchange, Delle had still called me by my nickname. Didn't that mean she still had feelings?

"Finn—e—gan!" The shrewd voice echoed through the castle's walls.

I cringed and blew out a sigh. "Yes, my Queen?"

"Where are you?" she boomed.

"Where do you *think* I am?"

And why was I having a conversation through the ice? Why couldn't she just appear and speak to me in person? Inwardly, I shook my head with disgust, though I'd never do it to her face. *Fairies.* I hated communicating with her this way. She probably only did it to get under my wings. Well, congratulations, Mom.

"Not by my side where you should be," she snapped. Her face materialized at the end of the hall, like a mirror. "Nor are you outside celebrating Winter. In fact, I haven't seen much of you at all these past few sundowns. Are you still sulking?" Most of her head disappeared, leaving behind only the narrowed slits of her eyes. "Forget about her and Summer. You are a Prince of Winter. *Act like it!*"

Her blue eyes blinked out, and I turned away, proceeding to the Great Hall. Now I'd have to show my face in court. How I hated this formal crap. No one cared about me, least of all the rest of her Winter subjects. They were too engrossed in the sword fights, the brawling, and the massive drinking to notice their Prince had arrived to grace them with his presence.

"Ah, there you are my sweet boy." Mab smiled when I walked into the Great Hall. "You have finally come to your senses." Before I could respond, she waved her hand, telling me she wasn't finished. "I thought I raised you better than that. Maybe you still need to be taught a lesson not to defy me."

"I have done nothing—"

"You're correct on that point." The smile was gone. "You have done nothing to make me proud. Not proud enough to call you a Prince of Winter, anyway."

"Good. Both of you are here." A male voice floated toward us from the sky, followed by an intense ray of light. The light created a perfect white circle, and a tall Angel appeared within it, dressed in a deep blue, gauzy robe. His feet were strapped into gold sandals, his magnificent gray wings still extended. He hovered in the air around us, surrounded by the light.

"Peace be with you," he said. "I am aware I'm not welcomed here, but I beg you hear me out."

There hadn't been any angels in Winter for a long time. Not since Mab had ordered them not to return to Aesculus Castle. This one was different. His feathers pulsed with a power that made me flinch.

Mab turned her back on the Angel. "Everyone has been correct lately: my son, and now you. Follow, if you wish to speak with us."

The Angel and I walked behind the Queen as she stormed into the throne room. So she wanted to impress him. I had my doubts, though. I wasn't sure anything would faze this angel, least of all seeing Mab sit on a slab of ice, trying to appear God-like.

"Speak or quit wasting my time," Mab hissed.

"I just came from Summer Court," the angel said gently. "King Oberon is deploying a team of fairies to search for The Redeemer."

"Who's that?" I asked.

"A human girl will be born, and she will save the world from Armageddon. The Summer King has spoken the Prophesy."

"What does it say, exactly?" Mab asked.

The angel cleared his throat and looked straight at the queen, concentrating on the words. "It says,

Glory!
Babe born.
First and last.
Heaven and unto Earth;
Receives the highest in jubilation.
Enlightens will unite; they shall band.
Triumph be if darkness is driven back.
Help found who love, the world will stand."

Mab shook her head, unimpressed. "Who says Armageddon is upon us? What will trigger it? And how can an Ordinary girl possibly save the world?"

The angel remained silent. Did he not know the answer or did he not want to interrupt Mab? I knew firsthand what happened when someone stopped her mid-sentence. Not that she would do that to the Angel, but ... Okay, maybe she would, just to prove she could. I doubted the angel would let it go that far, though. And who knew what powers this angel held.

"Sammael is locked in Hell now, but he will escape," the angel informed us. "Nothing can last forever."

"We do," I said.

"To an extent, yes, but in time things change." The angel glanced my way. "You of all should understand that."

"Meaning?" the queen asked, shooting me a look.

I shrugged, but an odd sense of guilt was building in my stomach. "I don't understand what you're talking about."

"You can't hide it anymore," the angel told me.

"Hide what?" Mab demanded. She stood and marched toward me. "Tell me, boy. What are you hiding?"

I backed up a couple of steps. "Nothing! I'm not hiding anything!"

"The angel says you are, so you must be. Angels don't tell untruths. Ever. So spill it or so help me …" He eyes narrowed further. "And this better not have anything to do with that Summer whelp, either."

I shook my head.

The Angel took that opportunity to change my world. "The Prince is no longer part of Winter," he said calmly. "He's part—"

"*No!*" I shouted, panicked. I took a deep breath. "I will tell her what happened."

The Angel smiled slightly and held out one arm, giving me the floor. Mab looked as if she wanted to rip my head off, but I had no choice. The truth had to come out. Maybe … just maybe it would be better if it was out in the open.

"The Summer Princess and I found a porta stone," I managed. "We traveled to the Ordinaries' realm, but since I am of Winter, the sun drained most of my Glamour. To save me, the Summer Princess infused part of her essence into me …" I took another deep breath and blurted out, "and now I think I might be part Summer."

Mab clenched her fists. "You *can't* be!" She looked from me to the angel, who only nodded, confirming my declaration.

Very slowly, Mab turned her now black eyes toward me. "I will tend to you later," she spat, then she glanced at our guest. "Back to the matter at hand, Angel. What is it you want me to do?"

"Send a team to scout for The Redeemer."

"And if I don't?"

"Sammael will rule over Earth, then he will find a way to break into Fairyland. I don't think you'll like what he would do to Winter."

That was not the right approach. I could have told him that.

"No," she snapped. "Just let him try. I will not send my subjects on a fruitless hunt. You are not a Prophet, Angel, and you cannot guarantee when this human girl will be born. The answer is no. I will not. Leave now so we may continue to celebrate Winter." The queen waved her hand, dismissing both him and me. As I turned, she added, "Oh, and son?"

I waited.

She curled her index finger, telling me to come to her. "Don't get any ideas. Your punishment, my son, will be to stay in Winter—in this castle, until I deem you are worthy." She wrapped her cold hand around my shoulder then squeezed her nails into my flesh. There was nothing I could do.

"Yes, my Queen."

I followed the angel out of the room, trying not to rub my shoulder. My skin throbbed where my mother had laid her hand on me, and a tingling sensation spread down my arm. When I was out of her view, I shook my hand, trying to free myself from the colder than normal feeling that slid toward my fingertips. I led the Angel to the castle's gate, slightly peeved at him for forcing me to tell my mother my secret. There had been no reason for her to *ever* find out, I didn't think. I had been doing fine on my own, learning how to deal with the changes.

"Just tell me why," I seethed. "What good did it do to tell her that I'm part Summer?"

"You will come to understand it later."

I stared at him, wishing I could read his thoughts. Then something occurred to me. "Is Sidelle one of the fairies that Oberon sent to search for The Redeemer?"

"Yes."

I frowned. "So she's putting herself in danger and running from me."

He shrugged. "Possibly both. But she is protected. She will find help eventually." The angel glanced over his shoulder as heavy footsteps echoed off the walls behind us. A troop of guards appeared, dressed in armor. "I must return to Heaven. My welcome here is on the verge of being tested."

"It's important to find The Redeemer, isn't it?" I asked.

His expression was one of understanding. "Yes, but what can you do if you're a prisoner in the castle with no way to escape?" He frowned, considering. "Tell me, would you help if you could?"

To help Sidelle and win her back, yes.

"Angel!" one of the guards yelled. "You're no longer welcome here. The Queen has ordered your removal."

"There is no need for yelling." The angel cupped his hands together then spread them wide. "I am leaving." In the next instant, an intense white light appeared then exploded into the air, taking the angel with it.

"Wait!" I yelled at the empty air. "Who are you?"

The Archangel Michael, I heard clearly in my mind.

Hello Reader!

I hope you enjoyed *Arrows & Angels (Enlighten Series, Novella)*. I have to tell you, getting into the mindset from a male perspective was fun. Many readers have told me: "Is this near the end for you and the series?" Maybe. I'll have to see where the writing journey takes me.

I'd love to hear from you. You can write me at kristinvanrisseghem.com,
visit me on the web at www.KristinVanRisseghem.com,

Follow me on Twitter @KVanRisseghem, like my Facebook Page: www.facebook.com/pages/Kristin-D-Van-Risseghem-Author, and you can join the Enlighten Series Street Team!!

Finally, I need to ask a favor. I'd love a review of *Arrows & Angels (Enlighten Series, Novella)*. Reviews can be tough to come by these days. If you have the time, please leave a review on the outlet where you purchased this book. Not a writer? Don't worry. Just a couple of sentences will do it.

Thank you so much for reading *Arrows & Angels (Enlighten Series, Novella)* and for spending time with me!!

Read On,
Kristin D. Van Risseghem, Author

Acknowledgements

Thank you to my husband, family, friends and all my author connections I've made over the years who continue to support me in my writing endeavor; thank you!

To my wonderful friend Angie, who provides me my sane moments when I need to bounce off ideas.

To the Querying Authors, The Sit Down and Shut Up Team, AAYAA Group, and the YA Rendezvous . . . you all inspire me to keep writing, answer my questions and are my cheering sections when I want to give up.

To my critique partners: Ann, Tiea, Genevieve, and Jena. You give me words of wisdom.

To my wonderful content editor: Tera Cuskaden and my line editor, Natalia Brothers. You help me create deeper characters we grew to love, set in a realistic, but still a make believe place.

A *HUGE* thank you to Angela for a fantastic cover with so much colors, sparkles and swirls!

THANK YOU!

~Kristin~

About the Author

USA Today bestseller and award-winning young adult author, Kristin D. Van Risseghem grew up in a small town along the Mississippi River with her parents and older sister. Currently, she lives in Minnesota with her husband and two Calico cats. Kristin also loves attending book clubs, going shopping, and hanging out with friends. She has come to realize that she absolutely has an addiction to purses and shoes. They are her weakness and probably has way too many of both.

In the summer months, Kristin can usually be found lounging on her boat, drinking an ice cold something. Being an avid reader of YA and Women's Literature stories, she still finds time to read a ton of books in-between writing. And in the winter months, her main goal is to stay warm from the Minnesota cold!

Kristin's books are published by Kasian Publishing LLC